PRAISE FOR CARLA M. WILSON'S
IMPOSSIBLE CONVERSATIONS

"The underlying implication of Wilson's work is profound and should be appreciated by working artists and readers alike..."
—AMERICAN BOOK REVIEW

"By way of Wilson's splendid imagination, curious encounters guaranteed." —Edith Doove

"What a sublime achievement!" —Eckhard Gerdes

CURIOUS
IMPOSSIBILITIES

Carla M. Wilson

Introduction by

James R. Hugunin

BLACK SCAT BOOKS
2017

CURIOUS IMPOSSIBILITIES
Ten Cinematic Riffs
by Carla M. Wilson

Copyright © 2017 by Carla M. Wilson

Introduction © 2017 by James R. Hugunin

ISBN 13 978-0-9992622-0-7

Cover montage & book design by Norman Conquest

Cinema icons courtesy of Glyphish

BLACK SCAT BOOKS
Sublime Art & Literature
BlackScatBooks.net

For my Dad

CONTENTS

INTRODUCTION

by James R. Hugunin

The concealed essence of a phenomenon [herein, film] is often given by the past events that have happened to it, so that a concealed force continues to operate upon a phenomenon [film] as a kind of transcendental memory.
— Philip Goodchild, *Deleuze and Guattari* (1996)

True aesthetic innovation can only come from reworking and transforming existing imagery, ripping it from its original context and feeding it into new circuits of analogy.
—Andrew V. Uroskie, *"Beyond the Black Box"*

I remember the ashtrays. God, the number of cigarettes they burned up in the movies in those days.
—"Don't Even Try, Sam," William H. Gass, in *Cinema Lingua, Writers Respond to Film*

I have been totally spellbound by cinema. Hitchcock, Max Ophuls, Bergman, Godard, Truffaut, Marker, Fellini, all have enriched my imagination. I take photographs. I've tried my hand at films. I've worked on the special effects in Hollywood films. I study the history of photography and film. I dig film noir. I write criticism. During its heyday, I read *Screen, Screen Education,* and *Cahiers du cinema,* religiously; carried Christian Metz's *The Imaginary Signifier* (1977) around like some people do the Bible. Now I write fiction, fiction influenced by film.

Early on, I noticed that the interaction between film and literature has been a rich one — writing influencing film, film influencing writing. An example of the latter I encountered in college was American writer John Dos Passos's *U.S.A.* trilogy, which makes use of the language of the new medium of film and its supposed objectivity to convince readers of the veracity of his writing.

Dos Passos was writing during the decade when the aesthetic of New Objectivity dominated painting, photography, and cinema. He uses the "Camera-eye" (recall Ukrainian filmmaker Dziga Vertov's term "Kino-eye" for his documentaries) to denominate fifty-one sections as objective views ("draining off the subjective" is how Dos Passos puts it) re-enforcing his trilogy as a document of American life. The "camera-eye" fragments, autobiographical stream of consciousness writing encourages the feeling that *you,* through the author's eyes, are a witness too, *you*

11

identify with that camera-eye. Then there are the *Trilogy*'s "Newsreels" sections, consisting of front page headlines and article fragments from various newspapers, as well as lyrics from popular songs.

An example of the former is, of course, filmmakers adapting novels to film, resulting in the development of the conventions of classical Hollywood realist cinema. Even Godard was citing Dostoevsky in his interviews. But after World War II, avant-garde art and fiction started influencing film. There was the American "underground cinema" railing against the standard narrative Hollywood film stressing, instead, subjectivity and non-linear narrative, creating "film poems" in which dreams, stream-of-consciousness, extreme montage, and so forth challenged the viewer's attention.

In France, Hitchcock's films, Hollywood "B-movies" and what became dubbed "film noir," were inspiring both writers and filmmakers. New Wave cinema was matched by the New Novel. (Robbe-Grillet managed to bridge both). Conventions were challenged or appropriated and refunctioned. It was a time of great creative vitality. I remember spending hours in a large dark room (no lit iPhones) intrigued by the new visions offered me by my soon-to-be favorite directors.

Recently, there has been a resurgence of interest in this era of art film, often driven by nostalgia, in which Brakhage, Bergman, Truffaut, Godard, Fellini, and others have played a major role. In France, Gilles Deleuzes's series of Bergsonian-influenced film studies *Cinema I: the movement image* (1983) and *C4inema 2: the time-image* (1985), eventually translated into English, became well-known in academia here. In 2002, the updated third edition of P. Adams Sitney's study of avant-garde cinema, *Visionary Film: The American Avant-Garde, 1943 - 2000*, was published, with its noteworthy positing of a polarity emerging in filmic practice then between the use of "trance forms/psycho-drama," and "graphic cinema." Sitney's 1970 anthology of film criticism from *Film Culture Reader* was also republished in 2000. Soon followed major retrospectives of films of that period. Across the country, artists and film buffs, fed by postmodernist appropriation theory and nostalgia, began to take notice, see possibilities.

Many contemporary artists began doing visual riffs on cinema. There were video installations (Bill Viola) and other recent postmodernist engagements with the concepts of spectatorship (emphasis on the audience rather than the artist/director) and the *tableau* foregrounded: Jeff Wall's large still photograph, *Movie Audience* (1979), Thomas Struth's photographs of museum-goers, such as *Audience 2, Florence* (2004), the glass-factory *tableau* staged early into Werner Herzog's *Heart of Glass* (1976), Peter Greenaway's "Darwin" (1993), as well as the suspense-draining time-stretch of Hitchcock's original 105 minutes to 24 hours in Douglas Gordon's *24-Hour Psycho* (1993) meant to inspire viewers to see the original film with fresh eyes and, finally, the slow pans across near-static scenes projected large onto three walls by Chicago artists Yoni Goldstein and Meredith Zielke in their installation, *The Jettisoned Project* (2011), which makes one hyperconscious of movement, topology and time, creating an illusion one is *inside* time, inhabiting a sort of "time-machine," expanding seconds into minutes.

An analogous engagement, a u-turn back to film history and the great *auteurs*, has arisen within contemporary literature. New York-based (Westchester county) writer

INTRODUCTION

Yuriy Tarnawsky, in *Claim to Oblivion* (2016), admits to being deeply influenced by film, especially Buñuel (dream and memory), and offers insightful essays therein on Bergman's *Persona* (de-centered subject) and Antonioni's *L'eclisse* (the famous last seven-minute visual riff). Another essay in his book, giving insight into his own writing, is devoted to "adopting static images to narration," and mentions Georges Perec's use of such in his *Life: A User's Manual* (1978). In 2004, Bard University's periodical *Conjunctions:42: Cinema Lingua, Writers Respond to Film* (Spring issue) featured writers of such stature as William H. Gass, Joyce Carol Oates, and John Yau riffing on cinema. For instance, one of Yau's poems included therein is titled "Coming Attractions: Bela Lugosi contemplates all the movies he never made."

It is within this exciting context of aesthetic exchange between literature and film, theory and nostalgia, that we are now offered Carla M. Wilson's literary homage to key directors of significant art films, *Curious Impossibilities: Ten Cinematic Riffs*. In her "viewer-response" approach to riffing on film, Wilson mines the potential of riffing on post-modern literary theory's "reader-response" and "reception aesthetic" analyses of texts rooted in Roland Barthes' groundbreaking 1977 declamation that, "A text's unity lies not in its origin but in its destination . . . The birth of the reader *[viewer]* must be at the cost of the death of the Author *[Director]*. Appropriately, Wilson's clever riff on Robbe-Grillet begins with a quote from him: "Trust the spectator and make a film in which, past and present, memory and reality, fact and fiction are juxtaposed without transition or explanation."

Ms. Wilson, a film aficionado, re-functions pre-existing film scenes/dialogues, such that one could retitle Wilson's efforts here as *Ten Cinematic Riffs: The Birth of the Viewer as Re-writer*. Just as Pictures Generation photographer Richard Prince, a quintessential postmodern appropriationist, took pre-existing advertising imagery and "re-photographed" it to new effect, so does Wilson appropriate and re-write filmic material from her chosen beloved directors/films and developing a fragmented narrative, which the book's editor, Norman Conquest, has keenly visualized in his cover design.

Wilson's fragmented narrative strategies plays on the "tough dialogue" of film noir, of Godard's scripts, and the radical jump-cuts of New Wave, while also giving homage to her mentor, experimental writer Harold Jaffe. Jaffe's writing often originates in news reports from disparate sources that Jaffe "treats" in a technique he has described as "inserting a line or two, or rearranging the format, or simply setting the original text in a different context, not altering the figure but the ground," as seen in *Induced Coma: 50 & 100 Word Stories* (2014), in which his language is at its tersest.

Ms. Wilson has spoken of her passion for film; how childhood remembrances of her father waxing eloquent over old movie houses, hours spent watching everything from newsreels, to Buck Rogers, to film noir, to Hitchcock thrillers. His fascination became hers. Later, she and her father regularly went to the movies together. A father-daughter bond grew over shared cinematic experiences. They even attended lectures by the likes of Vincent Price, Orson Welles, and John Houseman. All later became important sources for a creative writing rooted in an early state of ecstatic development and connection with her father, something akin to what Virginia Woolf, referring to her own childhood experiences, called "the base upon which life stands." One thinks here of British novelist Henry Green, whose 1929 book, *Living*, is constructed of quick-fire editing and imagistic economy influenced by the cinema he addictively attended.

Wilson's early experiences (very similar to my own childhood introduction to great films by my cinephile father and my subsequent fascination with film noir and Hitchcock) were reactivated years later when she began her M.F.A. studies in writing, after completing a B.A. in Communications, fortuitously stumbling upon a Film and Fiction class that began to again focus her earlier interests in the "darkened room," but now directed onto a soon-to-be-exposed white screen of the writer's page.

Wilson does extensive research on the films and directors she's "played with" in these cinematic riffs. She watches the films over and over, taking meticulous notes on dialogue and scene, camera-eye and space. She seeks a point of entry into key aspects of each film. In her "take" on Fellini, she opens with a characteristic Fellini-esque setting that captures that director's skill at blending the real and the surreal:

> *A white, sandy beach stretches out before the camera, which pans slowly across a wide shot. Three small children are playing in the sand. A well-dressed man floats high above the beach, tethered at the ankle by a long length of rope, held loosely by another man below. The man on the beach is laughing, calling to the floating man to come down.*

Then she segues to Fellini strutting around with his megaphone, accosted by an Italian reporter querying, "Frederico, do you believe that life is like a film?" Then his producer worriedly asks, "We're going to begin soon, Fellini, where is your lead actress? Where is your cast?" That reporter goes on to ask the director about his shift from Neorealism "to filmmaking that was 'primarily oneiric'?" Further into the riff, Wilson has an American reporter ask about the director's intention in telling a story about a director's story; Fellini replies, "I hoped to convey three levels on which our mind lives: The past, the present, and the conditional . . . and of course, the realm of fantasy."

Wilson has here done more than give us a feeling for Fellini, evoking a nostalgic response — ah! those hilarious opening scenes of controlled chaos we associate with his films — but here she also introduces us readers to her location (a sandy beach, i.e., San Diego, where she lives), the critique of the objective god-perspective (the floating man who is chided to come down to earth), the terms of her engagement in her writing (the blending of fact and fiction, the element of time and memory), herself as author (the lead actress), and her characters (the cast). The initial riff, the Fellini riff, superbly introduces all the key terms of the whole book's aesthetic.

The next riff takes Andrei Tarkovsky's film *The Sacrifice* as a point of departure. The film's plot begins on the coast of Sweden with Aleksandr (Erland Josephson) celebrating his birthday with family and friends when they hear jets thundering overhead and receive stunning news from the radio. World War III has erupted, and the end of the world is near. In order to avert the apocalypse, Aleksander makes a bargain with God: He'll give up everything he values in life, including his beautiful home and beloved, but mute, son (Tommy Kjellqvist). So, eventually, Aleksander sets about doing just that. He tricks the family members and friends into going for a walk, and sets fire to their house when they are away. As the group rushes back, alarmed by the fire, Alexander confesses that he set the fire himself, and furiously runs around. Maria, their maid, who until then was not seen that morning, appears in the fire scene. Aleksander tries to approach her, but is restrained by others. Without explanation, an ambulance appears in the area and two paramedics chase Aleksander, who appears to have lost control of himself, and drive him off. Maria begins to bicycle away, but stops halfway to observe Little Man, the mute son, watering the dead tree he and Aleksander planted the day before. As Maria leaves the scene, Little Man, lying at the foot of the tree, speaks his only line, which quotes the opening Gospel of St. John: "In the beginning was the Word *[and after that there is only the Quote?]*. Why is that, Papa?"

The main themes Wilson plays with in her Tarkovsky piece are: fragments/collage/circus/ impending war/madness/too much talk/map and territory. In a section subtitled "MAPS AND TRUTH," one character, Otto, says "Maps reflected humanity's true view of the world." To which Aleksandr sniffs and replies "Truth . . . maps have nothing to do with truth," i.e,. films are purely constructs. Which brings to mind Polish-American scientist and philosopher Alfred Korzybski's famous remark that "the map is not the territory" and that "the word is not the thing," encapsulating his view that an abstraction derived from something, or a reaction to it, is not the thing itself. Korzybski held that many people do confuse maps with territories, that is, confuse models of reality with reality itself. Wilson, through Tarkovsky, brings up the epistemological status of filmic representation, and by extension her own writing.

In the short section on (Marguerite) Duras, scriptwriter on Alain Resnais' *Hiroshima mon amour*, Wilson has REALITY dialogue with MEMORY. This creative response to the film creates a nice segue to the next section, a response to Robbe-Grillet's paean to time and memory, *Last Year at Marienbad*.

Wilson's section on Robbe-Grillet's film was culled from a study of both the book and the movie. In it, two interlocutors (X = Man, A = Woman) go through three repeated cycles of dialogue and setting, each with small variations, mirroring the filmic device the author/director used to evoke differing memories rooted in the experience of different subjects (no god perspective here). As these dialogues progress then repeat, I found myself visually retrieving those scenes from the original film, vividly seeing myself in the very theatre where I first experienced this film, even sensing the presence of my then girlfriend beside me, our excited discussion after the viewing.

Alphaville, Godard's celebration of the sci-fi/noir genres — one of my favorite films — is a dystopia where there is an absence of beauty, truth, and love. To say the word "love" is punishable by pain. It is celebrated by Wilson's excellent mimicry of the tone of the dialogue and stark scenes in Godard's dark masterpiece. Her text and Godard's film (Lemmy Caution you!) interweave like a helix of recombinant DNA. In the film, in Wilson's riff, life and death are interwoven: "Natacha: This evening we learned that life and death exist all within the same circle." Natacha is the daughter of scientist Von Braun, the creator of Alpha 60, a computer that uses mind control to rule over residents of Alphaville and who the secret agent Lemmy C. is teamed up with against her father. At one point, Natacha says, "The words seem oddly familiar, but I'm still not sure what they mean," a wonderful nod to the film, a self-reference to

Wilson's own text, and to the quandary of the discourse coming out of Washington these days. The dystopian theme of the film is even more relevant today, given our current President and the rise of the Alt-Right, than when it was released.

Mirroring Wilson's play on her own appropriation of pre-existing fragments is her choice to riff on Chris Marker's film *San Soleil*. This experimental film by French director Chris Marker (of *La Jetée* fame) collects stock footage recorded in various countries around the world and presents it in collage-like form, using no synchronized sound, but instead ties the various segments together with music and voice-over narration, which ponders the topics such as memory, technology and society. Expanding the documentary genre, this experimental essay-film is a composition of thoughts, images and scenes, mainly from Japan and Guinea-Bissau, two extreme poles of our global condition. Other scenes were filmed in Cape Verde, Iceland, Paris, and San Francisco. As a female narrator reads from letters supposedly sent to her by the (fictitious) cameraman Sandor Krasna, Wilson describes her character: "She took a sketchbook and a camera with her everywhere." Here we see how appropriate this film is as it plays upon the role Wilson herself has taken *vis-à-vis* her filmic material in the whole book.

The Truffaut section, a witty riff on *Day for Night*, was well chosen. I think it's the best of all the sections. The title in French is *La Nuit Américaine* (*American Night*), a term for using film stock balanced for indoor tungsten light outdoors in the daytime, underexposed, then futzed with in post-production to simulate night scenes. Day for night may be, then, understood as a code for filmic simulation, deceit, the collapse of any distinction between the real and the fictional, a blurring of sharp distinctions, an attack on binary thinking. This section is appropriately prefaced with a quote by the director: "I have always preferred the reflection of the life to life itself." Wilson takes this section's inspiration from the friendship between the key innovators of New Wave cinema, Truffaut and Godard, and their later conflict and falling out, the cord between them decisively severed after the release of Truffaut's immensely popular *Day for Night*, which Godard found to be dishonest and told Truffaut as much in the first of a series of angry letters between the two men.

For all his radical Marxist politics, Godard in his feud with Truffaut, comes off like a Fascist. Given the current tendency toward "fascism of the Left" in many of our institutions, Wilson's point to make something of Godard's elitist snobbery, hits home, but does so humorously, a true-*faux-pas*. How? She gives Godard a cameo appearance in her narrative riff. In fact, a Truffaut fan and a Godard fan take potshots at each other in the narrative. A narrative that begins with an excited Spectator #1 declaiming, "Cool, we get to watch a film being filmed!" His interlocutor, Spectator #2, replies, "It's a film about filmmaking." (Here my thoughts flew back to Dziga Vertov's film about filmmaking, *The Man with the Movie Camera*.) This is, of course, a reference to what Wilson herself is doing and what the reader also experiences when reading this re-writing of Truffaut in this section. What the spectators are discussing is the film-within-the-film, a *mise-en-abyme* scene showing the filming and directing of a film inside the main film titled *Je Vous Présente Pamèla* (*Meet Pamela*) occurring within *Day for Night* (search YouTube for a clip of this scene).

In the Ershadi section, Wilson takes as her starting point Homayoun Ershadi's friendship with Iranian New Wave director Abbas Kiarostami and the latter's 1997 award-winning film *Taste of Cherry*. In the story a Mr. Badii (played by Ershadi) is a man in a Range Rover driving through the wastelands outside Tehran, crisscrossing a barren industrial landscape of construction sites and shanty towns, populated by young men looking for work. The driver picks up a young serviceman, asking him, at length, if he's looking for work: "If you've got money problems, I can help." Is this a homosexual pickup? Kiarostami deliberately allows us to draw that inference for a time, all the while offering "red herrings" to mislead the spectator, before gradually revealing the true nature of the job, someone who can carry out the task of burying him after he commits suicide. Wilson's conceit here is to herself play a role, that of an interviewer of Ershadi on set after filming has concluded. Asking HE why his character takes so long to find just the right person for the grisly task, HE replies that every person Mr. Badii encounters spans a cross-section of humanity: "Ultimately, in my view, is about having a choice and having a voice. . . . By using every-day people as actors the director gives us an undistilled version of culture that is embodied in the individual, even as s/he is part of a collective society. . . . Even in the depths of sadness or despair, we may still see a glimmer of light at the end of the tunnel *[the light projected onto the screen?]* when we remember the taste of cherry *[sweet memories of films viewed?]*."

Responding to CW's questions, Ershadi talks about his long friendship with Kiarostami. Ershadi has offered his friend (off set) a cigarette, a gesture that also showed up in the last "controversial scene of the film," of which CW asks HE: "Was it intentionally included?" and HE replies, "Yes, Mr. Kiarostami wanted the familiarity between us shown. He wanted the audience to get a sense of real life continuing even as the film, and perhaps my character's life, concluded." Again, Wilson invites us into an awareness of the blurred line between reality and fiction rooted, I believe, in Wilson's early formative experiences in moving into and out of that dark room, the movie theatre, in and out of dream and reality until they began to merge in her imagination. It is this dialectic — realized in dialogue — that interests this very talented author.

In concluding this essay, let me cite at length CW asking HE about the film's conclusion and HE's response:

> CW: *So what about the conclusion? Why does Mr. K. [Kiarostami] bring us all the way to the end, to the scene where Badii lies in his grave in the rain, only to have the screen go black?* [This particular scene recalls to mind a similar, but more comic one, in Russian director Aleksandr Medvedkin's early silent film *Happiness*, where a forlorn, abused kulak jumps into a coffin and refuses to come out.] . . . *We have come all this way, became involved with Badii's narrative, only to find that the climactic build up provides no relief ... we are faced with the reality that, yes, we are watching a film, and the entire film has been a construct of the director's imagination.*

> HE: *Yes, the film is a construct. In this way, you can compare Mr. K.'s film-making to conceptual art. There are no concrete answers. . . .*

CW: Yes. And next we see the film crew and the director, and you giving your friend, Mr. K., the cigarette.

Can we not read into this a thinly veiled allusion to Wilson's own project where concrete interpretations elude us and polysemy reigns? Isn't she, both actor and director in these riffs, handing us, too, a "cigarette" in a friendly gesture of readerly collaboration?

My final critical word concerning Wilson's achievement in this book?

Smokin'!

James R. Hugunin is an Adjunct Full Professor in the Department of Art History, Theory, and Criticism at The School of the Art Institute of Chicago. In 1983, he won the Reva and David Logan Award for Distinguished New Writing in Photography. He also writes experimental fiction.

FELLINI

CIRCUS

SETTING

A white, sandy beach stretches out before the camera, which pans slowly across a wide shot. Three small children are playing in the sand. A well-dressed man floats high above the beach, tethered at the ankle by a long length of rope, held loosely by another man below. The man on the beach is laughing, calling to the floating man to come down.

FADE IN:

An expansive movie set bustling with activity: characters in costume move back and forth across the scene, a brass band is playing, a man wearing a clown costume wanders by, followed by a dancer in a skimpy outfit preening in her large feathered and be-jeweled headdress. Photographers and reporters stalk their prey like hunted animals.

FELLINI enters the set carrying a megaphone. He is wearing a large, black hat. He is immediately accosted by a reporter.

Italian Reporter: Frederico, do you believe that life is like a film?

Producer: We're going to begin soon, Fellini, where is your lead actress? Where is your cast?

French Actress: What part am I playing?

Fellini (to reporter): The answer to your question is complex…

Producer: You use too much symbolism; you need to cut it out.

Photographer: Mr. Fellini, may we get a shot of you? Please, look into the camera and smile. That's right. Take off your sunglasses. [FLASH!]

Italian Reporter: Could we return to my interview, please? Is it true that Carl Jung's autobiography "Memories, Dreams, Reflections," (1963) influenced you?

Fellini: Indeed. My psychoanalyst recommended it.

American Reporter: Ernst Bernhard was your psychoanalyst. Didn't he also recommended you consult the I-Ching?

Fellini: And keep a record of my dreams, yes, true.

Italian Reporter: Care to explain further?

Photographer: Just another shot, please; stand here with Claudia Cardinale, if you wouldn't mind? [Snap, snap] that's it…Claudia, head back please, open your blouse a little more, there, like that….Fellini, take off those sunglasses!

Fellini: What I formerly accepted as my "extrasensory perceptions" were eventually interpreted as psychic manifestations of the unconscious.

Italian Reporter: So Bernhard's suggestion that you focus on Jungian depth psychology proved to be the single greatest influence on your mature style and marked the turning point in your work from Neorealism to filmmaking that was "primarily oneiric"?

Fellini: I, I…

French Actress: Frederico! Please tell me what my character's motivation is! I must inhabit my character and therefore need as much time as possible to reflect upon who she really is…But you haven't told me one thing!

Producer: Frederico, who are these people? We need to get the script polished up. We are meeting with the promoters soon and they mustn't be kept waiting! When is the soundman arriving?

Clown: Do you like my hat?

French Actress: How do you like mine?

Italian Reporter: Consequently, Jung's seminal ideas on the anima and the animus, the role of archetypes, and the collective unconscious directly influenced such films as *8 1/2*, *Juliet of the Spirits*, *Satyricon*, *Casanova*, and *City of Women*, I would imagine.

Fellini: True.

French Actress: Why am I even here? I haven't even been told what my part is…

American Reporter: Could you please explain what *8 ½* is about? There is so much ambiguity I can't follow the story!

Fellini: It's about a director who wanted to make a film he no longer remembers. It's a film telling the story of a director who no longer knows what film he wanted to make…

Italian Reporter: Ahhh, the creative process comes to mind here…Was there much improvisation?

French Actress: I'll say there was.

American Reporter: Please, tell us what your intention was in telling this director's story?

Fellini: I hoped to convey three levels on which our mind lives: The past, the present, and the conditional…and of course, the realm of fantasy.

Clown: And dreams? What about dreams?

Claudia Cardinale: The dream world figures prominently in his work, of course! It also functions through symbolic gestures and characters. My character is the symbol of purity and light, redemption and truth.

Producer: He uses too many archetypes and symbols. Nobody gets it!

Claudia Cardinale: Did you know Frederico became increasingly attracted to parapsychology and was introduced to the work of Spiritism and Seances which influenced his later work?

American Reporter: I don't understand at all what he was trying to say. I can't follow the narrative!

Fellini: I wanted to free my work from certain constrictions. I didn't want to make a story with a beginning, a development, an ending. I wanted my work to be more like a poem with metre and cadence...

Clown: Fellini was also a talented studio artist.

Italian Reporter: I didn't know that!

Clown: Yes, he had an exhibit of 63 drawings in 1982 in Paris, Brussels, and a gallery in New York.

Italian Reporter: What were they?

Clown: Caricatures, mostly, drawings derived from and inspired by his own dreams.

Claudia Cardinale: What did I tell you?

American Reporter: Is it true that in 1984 you met Carlos Castaneda, the Peruvian writer of "Don Juan: A Yaqui Way of Knowledge"?

Fellini: Yes, I accompanied him to the Yucatan to assess the feasibility of a film.

Italian Reporter: What happened?

Fellini: He disappeared on me.

Clown: Went off into the jungle somewhere and was never to be heard from again! Frederico was pretty peeved and ended up making a film that was a satire of one of Castaneda's Don Juan books.

Dwarf: I heard he took LSD.

Clown: Castaneda or Fellini?

Producer: That's enough, that's enough now...We're shooting next week! I need everybody to get ready!

Fellini: I wonder what the point of it all is...

American Actress: Why, the solitude of modern man in contemporary cinema, of course!

Older Dancer with Feathered Headdress: Only the man's dreams are important, as usual. I always knew my days were numbered! This is about the young replacing the old, isn't it? You're going to make me go upstairs, aren't you?

Fellini: You knew the rules when you accepted the job!

Older Dancer with Feathered Headdress: I'll revolt! I deserve to be loved until I'm seventy!

Priest: You mustn't mistreat women, Frederico.

Fellini: Frankly, I don't really care anymore whether the audience understands my work.

American Actress: How can you not care?

Doctor: You're overworked. Go to the spa and undwind.

Priest: His eminence is waiting for you in the mudbaths, Fellini. You must confess everything. Get in his good graces for us.

Editor: You say you want to bring order, clarity, truth to this narrative, but now you're bringing in a Catholic polemic?

Italian Reporter: I was raised Catholic, too, by the way. Where are we going with this?

Priest: Childhood memories, Catholic consciousness, confession, confirmation. All part of the story.

Claudia Cardinale: The ultimate goal for Frederico is to find the perfect girl who can help him begin again with a clean slate.

Clown: Remember Mallarmé's "White Page"? Nothingness.

French Actress: Nothingness! C'est impossible!

Zen Monk: Nothingness is the sound of one hand clapping.

Fellini: Your Emminence, all I wanted to do was to make an honest film, something simple and helpful to people. Where are the spirit messengers now? They have all abandoned me. I have nothing left to say.

Cardinal: You're trying to solve a problem for which there are no answers. You are trying to find clarity in the faces of characters you could never love. The best thing to do is to tell the truth.

Dwarf: 'Characters he could never love'? These are characters he could never create. He just appropriated them, if you want to know the truth.

Luisa, Fellini's Wife: He tells the truth as it suits him. Lies while swearing he's telling the truth. He can't even tell the truth to the woman who has grown old by his side, I tell you.

Fellini: Luisa, I love you.

Luisa: He doesn't even know how to love.

French Actress: He certainly doesn't!

Doctor: You're overworked, Fellini. Has the spa-treatment helped?

Photographer: Just a moment, please, look over here: [FLASH!]

Claudia Cardinale: Please, I'm here to help. Just let me help you.

Fellini: Claudia, you've arrived just in time. You are the girl of my dreams, the girl who can purify me, the girl who passes out the healing water in the beginning of the film, but I cannot let you help me because I have nothing left to give you in return.

Claudia Cardinale: He meets a girl who can give him new life and he pushes her away?

American Reporter: Can anybody tell me what he is trying to say?

Clown: We are all smothered by words, images, sounds that have no meaning or no right to exist. They come from the void and should return to the void.

Dwarf: What can he hope to achieve by stringing together his own tattered memories and mistakes if he creates characters he could never love?

French Actress: Existential truths, of course!

Fellini: Suddenly I am happy. I see the truth about love and acceptance of myself and my confusion, and I understand that all this confusion is my own alone. The most important thing for me to ask of you now is for you to accept me as I am, and I in turn must accept you as you are and love you for who you are. I want to live life, to celebrate it. Love is so simple! Love, truth and acceptance are all we need.

Producer: We're about to begin filming! Fellini! Where is everybody? Are you ready?

Photographer: Just one more shot, look over here (snap-snap-snap) and please take off those sunglasses!

[FLASH!]

TARKOVSKY

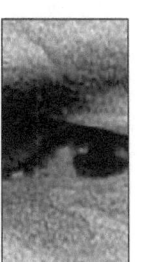

THE SACRIFICE

Alexander: "I've waited for this all my life. My whole life has been one long wait for this." — *The Sacrifice*

SETTING

On the coast of Sweden, there is a large two-story house by the sea. Aleksandr and his little boy are crouched near the shore, attempting to plant a dead tree into a hole in the ground.

DIALOGUE

"Water the tree until it comes to life," Aleksandr tells the boy.

"For three years a monk watered his dead tree and one day it came to life. See? Perform the same act, a ritual, every day and it will come true. It could change the world."

"If he truly believes, it will be so," said the boy.

"Humanity is on the wrong road," said Aleksandr. "Everyone should be silent, like you. Did you know: Ghandi didn't speak to anyone for an entire week. It didn't bother him."

"I'm not afraid to die," said the boy.

"There is no such thing as Death" (says Aleksandr to the boy).

"It seems to me," said the boy, "that any progress we make is inevitably turned into evil. I find civilization to be defective."

"What's that you say? Evil? Sin? Corruption? What, then, is the solution?"

"It's too late," said the boy. "I'm weary of talk. Words, words, words. I wish everyone would stop talking and do something instead."

DREAM SEQUENCE (BLACK AND WHITE):
Water dripping, eerie singing, a birch forest… The little boy disappears, then sneaks up on him in a playful way. Aleksandr turns and accidentally knocks the boy over, giving him a nose bleed. Aleksandr feels terrible.

JUMP CUT:
The house. Aleksandr's birthday. He is given an art book of religious icons: spiritual, childlike, profound, prayer-like. He feels his life is a failure despite that he is well-educated: he has studied history, philosophy, and has been an accomplished writer, but he feels he has put himself in prison with all of his knowledge. An actor's identity dissolves in the roles he plays, he says.

Creaking noises, birds, floorboards, doors creaking, the sound of wind chimes…

OTTO

Otto the postman gives Aleksandr a rare map of Europe from the 1600s.

"Every gift involves a sacrifice."

MARIA

Maria, the servant-girl from Iceland, is said to be a witch. She is instructed by Aleksandr's wife to light the candles, warm the plates, open the wine before dinner; then she may be allowed to go home.

MAPS AND TRUTH

"Do you see?" says Otto, "Maps reflected humanity's true view of the world."

"Truth…" sniffs Aleksandr, "…maps have nothing to do with truth, but thank you, nevertheless."

"Here is something to cheer you up," says Otto: "I collect incidents!"

"What do you mean, 'incidents'?" says Aleksandr.

"I mean the unexplainable," says Otto. "I have collected 284 incidents which cannot be explained. I need a lot of time to make sure they are true, however."

Otto collapses suddenly.

"An evil angel passing by me who saw fit to mess with me." Maria crosses the moors.

JUMP CUT:
The glasses in the cabinets rattle, an airplane's engine roars above, shakes the house, breaks things.

The boy is asleep in his room upstairs. The room has only one bed, one window.

Adoration of the three kings by Leonardo is "sinister" to Otto. He is terrified of Leonardo.

Japanese flute music plays.

News comes on the television about the impending war.

WAITING

"Our only enemy is order against chaos," the news announcer says.

The family is in the sitting room watching the news on TV: *warheads, missiles, warnings about war, the phone is continually ringing, television lights are blinking, suddenly: darkness, mist, silence. Black and white images flash upon the screen.*

Alexander: "I've waited for this all my life. My whole life has been one long wait for this."

Long takes, silence.

Viktor (a friend of the family, a doctor) gives the hysterical mother and daughter sedatives. Alexander has a drink instead, waiting for the apocalypse.

The boy sleeps upstairs.

Windchimes. Alexandr learns the telephone line is dead.

PRAYING

The boy's mother: "Why do we always do the opposite of what we want? We simply don't want to depend on each other. Men and women love differently. One weak, the other strong. We fight against ourselves, against something we don't want to give in to; we say to ourselves: don't go along with anything or you'll die…"

Alexander prays and vows to relinquish everything if only God would restore everything to the way it was the day before. He fears that there will be no birds, no water in the wells, no cities, no towns, no cities or people. Then he goes to sleep under the painting of the Maji.

The older daughter tries to seduce Viktor, her mother's lover.

The sirens sing.

CUT TO:
A room with one bed, one painting; one window.

DREAM SEQUENCE:
Water dripping, sirens singing, gauze curtains blowing, snow, mud, black and white images, water, mud, leaves. Aleksandr crosses the field in the snow. He sees the naked girl. Goes to

follow her. Sirens singing, forests of birch trees, leaves, coins, money, wet clothing. He dreams of his little boy asleep in his room. Then: a brick wall with a door covering it. The painting of the Maji.

DENOUMENT: ONE CHANCE

Otto wakes him: *"There is still one chance: one hope* (is it still a dream?)*"*; he tells him he must go to see Maria, his servant girl, and convince her to lie with him. She lives on a farm on the other side of the bay, behind the church. He must go to Maria so that everything can be over and done with. *"Lie with her. You must make a wish at that moment and then everything will be over."* Aleksandr doesn't believe him, thinks Otto is having a trick. *"She is a witch…in the best sense. There is no other alternative."* He must take Otto's bike. He prefers Piero Della Francesca he says at last before he goes (over the Leonardo painting of the three Maji).

NARRATIVE ASIDE:

Is it possible for man to become art? The actor himself is his own creation, his own work of art. But he is only an actor.

SALVATION / THE CLIMAX

Aleksandr climbs down the ladder behind the house after checking on the boy and sees his family seated at a table with a lamp on it. Aleksandr's wife, daughter, and Viktor, are at a table on the beach dressed in Victorian clothing. The table is set in Victorian décor.

Aleksandr takes Otto's bicycle and rides behind the barn so they don't see him. He rides the bike frantically down the dirt path, towards the end of the fields. Exhausted, he falls over a couple of times, but carries on.

He finds Maria's house. She lets him in. She has religious items on her shelf: a cross, a vase of flowers, photographs of her parents, and otherwise the room is empty with nothing on the walls. There is a table with flowers, a lamp a chair, a piano. She asks him if everything is ok at his house.

Aleksandr asks if Maria has a TV, if she has heard the news. He has hurt his hands, falling off the bike. She washes his hands in the bowl with soap and water, and the vase: pours water over them. Afterwards, he sits and plays a melancholy tune on the piano. There is a cross on the wall. He says he played this prelude as a child, and his mother loved it. His mother's house was in the country. It had a little untended garden. He used to visit her there when she was ill. There was something beautiful about the untended garden. She would sit at the window and look out at it. One day he wanted to tidy up the garden to please her. He went at it for two weeks, even as his mother's condition grew worse. When he was finished, he wanted to show his mother her new garden. He took a bath and got dressed in his finest clothes. He took a look at the garden from her chair and was disappointed at what he saw: the naturalness, the beauty was gone. The violence of it. His sister had cut her hair once, and his father had been disappointed in a similar way.

Aleksandr asks Maria to "love him" and "save us all." She tells him to go home. She has a bicycle too; she could ride with him. He puts a gun to his head. She takes pity on him, tells him there is nothing to fear, tells him not to cry.

CUT TO:
An overturned car and people running, a Japanese flute; eerie singing.

While they lie together, Aleksandr cries and cries. Maria calms him and holds him– he sees his family in his mind and wants to go to them. He wakes up on the same couch back at home where he had last seen Otto.

"Maria…?"

Japanese flute music is playing on the JVC stereo in a cabinet. There is also a mirror.

CONCLUSION
The phone, which had been out of order just last evening works in the morning. Aleksandr calls his office to make sure. He asks if everything is ok there: the office seems to be busy; business as usual, and nothing is mentioned about the war. He looks into the boy's room – it looks empty – the lamp works again – it all appears to have been a bad dream. The ladder is still there on the side of the house, however, leading up to his window.

FINAL SCENE
The daughter tells her mother that Viktor is not coming back, that he is going to Australia. The mother, who loves Viktor, becomes hysterical, asking why. Viktor says he's *"tired of the lot of you. Tired of being your nursemaid and your warden."*

They argue, and decide to start walking to the beach after finding a strange letter left to them by Aleksandr. They talk about his affinity for everything Japanese.

The boy is already far away from them, near the shore at the Japanese tree.

Aleksandr is wearing a kimono with a black and white yin/yang symbol on the back. He stacks up all the wicker chairs and lights a tablecloth on fire (to help ignite the flames). He had promised he'd give up everything if God would make everything OK.

He turns on the Japanese flute music very loud - wearing the kimono – the music plays. He sits for a moment and has a drink, then climbs down the ladder as the house he loves begins to burn.

His family all come running back from the beach when they see the fire.

Aleksandr shouts "I did it! I've got something very important to say: Be silent, water the tree, and all will be well."

The phone is ringing.

Maria the witch arrives and Aleksandr kneels reverently at her feet. Maria tries to tell everyone to leave Alexandr be. Viktor calls an ambulance and several men in white coats arrive and chase Alexandr (who runs away like a madman) across the field until he is caught and put him in the ambulance.

Maria takes the bike and rides off down the road towards

where the boy is at the shore.

The whole house burns to the ground while Alekandr's family looks on in dismay and disbelief.

The boy is at the Japanese tree, watering it.

Maria greets the ambulance and the boy near the tree, while a high-pitched voice calls to a group of cows which are silently grazing in the field.

The boy waters the tree, Maria stands with the bicycle for a moment and watches the ambulance drive by the tree. She rides off, across the moors…

DURAS

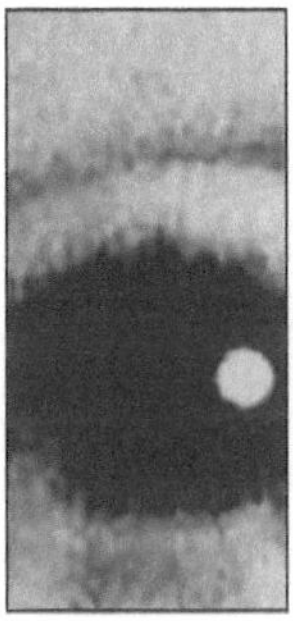

HIROSHIMA – THE TWIN

"I think about you but I don't say it anymore."
—Marguerite Duras, Hiroshima Mon Amour

[REALITY]

In bed next to me, my twin puts her hands over her ears, listening to her heartbeat, her own breathing—tells me what she hears.

"I meet you. I remember you. Who are you? You're destroying me. You're good for me. How could I know this city was tailor-made for love? How could I know you fit my body like a glove? I like you. How unlikely. I like you. How slow all of a sudden. How sweet. You cannot know. You're destroying me. You're good for me. You're destroying me. You're good for me. I have time. Please, devour me. Deform me to the point of ugliness. Why not you? Why not you in this city and in this night, so like other cities and other nights you can hardly tell the difference? I beg of you."

[MEMORY]

"He and I are together, in France, walking," she says. "We stand, looking at the countryside. We kiss; embrace. The sky is on fire, striped in evening pink, orange, black. Merciful clouds scatter raindrops into the porous earth. We kiss; embrace. It begins to rain harder. We argue over nothing. We go back inside.

He drapes his coat upon the wooden chair and pours me a strong drink. I put on music and light a match to start the fire. He lights a cigarette. We drink our drinks. The fire begins roaring, crackling. We go to bed."

Elle: *All these years I've been looking for an impossible love.*
Lui: *You were bored in a way that makes a man want to know a woman*

[REALITY]

My twin says the sound of her hands cupped over her ears is like the ocean breathing. Her pulse is slow and steady. She's feeling better now. Before, the pain had made her sit up, propped against a pillow. She heard voices. Couldn't slow her breathing. Felt a weight on her chest like an elephant.

An elephant is good luck, I say. She tells me she doesn't feel lucky; maybe she deserved to suffer. I say that's nonsense, let's go back to sleep. No reason to hate yourself. She asks whether I really think so. I say yes.

I had long hair then, she reminds me. They cut it off and threw me in the cellar to make me forget. I suppose I went mad because I loved him too much. He was on the other side, I remind her. He was forbidden.

"I meet you. I remember you. Who are you? You're destroying me. You're good for me. How could I know this city was tailor-made for love? How could I know you fit my body like a glove? I like you. How unlikely. I like you. How slow all of a sudden. How sweet. You cannot know. You're destroying me. You're good for me. You're destroying me. You're good for me. I have time. Please, devour me. Deform me to the point of ugliness. Why not you? Why not you in this city and in this night, so like other cities and other nights you can hardly tell the difference? I beg of you."

[MEMORY]

During the war we met secretly, as often as we could. My new lover is Japanese. We've only just met; and I'm leaving in the morning. I'm telling him all this as we drink together at the restaurant overlooking the river. He pours me another glass of beer and says he wants to know more about my lover because then he'll know more about who I am now. My Hiroshima was German, I explain; he was shot and killed somewhere along a country road as he was on his way to meet me. Then the war ended and I went to Paris.

Elle: I'm beginning to forget you. Forgetting so much love is terrifying.
Lui: Some years from now, when I have forgotten you and other romances like this one have recurred through sheer habit, I will remember you as a symbol of love's forgetfulness. This affair will remind me how horrible forgetting is.

He asks what I know of Hiroshima.

I've been to the museum, I say. I've seen photographs of the men, women and children left crippled in the aftermath. Burned faces, eyes, peeling skin, hair lost in clumps, deformed limbs. Animals, people, wandering like ghosts. I know what I saw. You saw nothing, he says.

Elle: Were you here in Hiroshima?
Lui: Of course not.
Elle: That's right. How silly of me.
Lui: But my family was in Hiroshima.
Lui: I was off fighting the war.
Elle: Lucky for you, eh?

Lui: *Yes.*
Elle: *Lucky for me, too.*

[REALITY]

My twin finally falls asleep and I hear her breathing. I try to remember my lover's face, but can't. I'm no longer the same as when I left for Paris. I didn't want to know anything more about my Japanese lover, I tell my twin.

[MEMORY]

I ask my lover if he was in Hiroshima when the bomb dropped. He tells me he wasn't, but his entire family had been there. How could I know anything about Hiroshima? I insist I saw everything; that I know Hiroshima, but he denies it is true. You are not endowed with memory, he says. When you speak, I wonder whether you lie or tell the truth. 'I lie…I say, 'and I tell the truth.'

When I try to shake him, he follows me all night, even when I sit with another man. I want to go back to my normal life; forget Nevers; forget Hiroshima. He sits down after the man leaves, putting his mouth to my ear. He thinks he loves me, he says. I am his Hiroshima.

ROBBE-GRILLET

X1

"Trust the spectator and make a film in which, past and present, memory and reality, fact and fiction are juxtaposed without transition or explanation."

NARRATOR:

We walked through the corridors, endless and baroque, with mirrors along the hallways and ornate mantle pieces in every room. Each room is just like the rest, one bedroom is just like another and you were there suddenly and you turned and said to me you wanted me to come to Marienbad again next year and as it turns out you had remembered that I was there the year before and remembered the statues and that I had asked you what the names of the statues were and wondered whether maybe they were falling off a cliff or about to fall off a cliff and you laughed but you never answered you only described them – they could be us for all you knew. I asked again what their names were and you gave two names of Greek gods and I laughed and we continued to speculate about what it was that they were doing. Was one running away from the other or were they playing a game? Was there ever a final embrace? You never answered. But the man who no one knew came and stood nearby watching us until I said I had to leave.

DIALOGUE:

A. I'm leaving.

X. Must you go already?

A. I must. He is waiting.

X. I wish you wouldn't.

A. I have to go now.

X. Must you really leave already?

A. I must. He is waiting.

X. I wish you wouldn't.

A. Leave me alone.

X. I cannot. You were here last year.

A. I could not have been here last year. It's impossible.

X. But you were here.

A. How do you know?

X. I remember it clearly. You wore a long white gown with feathers around your neck and wrists. You sat on the bed, waiting. Or was it black?

A. I never.

X. You sat on the bed and you waited.

A. Wearing a white dress with feathers?

X. A white swan. You could have been one of the white swans gliding quietly across the cold, black lake.

A. Waited for what? For whom? It's impossible.

X. Yet I remember it clearly. We were meant to meet again.

A. But you are implying we had already met once. We did not.

X. How can you explain this memory, then?

A. I'm leaving.

X. Must you leave already?

A. I must. He is waiting.

X. I wish you wouldn't.

A. Leave me alone.

X. I cannot. You were here last year.

Jazz, collage, memory, dream space. Is it a dream or is it not? Did something happen last year at Marienbad? Who is the man? Who is the woman, have they met?

NARRATOR:

We walked through the corridors, endless and baroque, with mirrors along the hallways and ornate mantle pieces in every room. Each room is just like the rest, one bedroom is just like another and you were there suddenly and you turned and said to me you wanted me to come to Marienbad again next year and as it turns out you had remembered that I was there the year before and remembered the statues and that I had asked you what the names of the statues were and wondered whether maybe they were falling off a cliff or about to fall off a cliff and you laughed but you never answered you only described them – they could be us for all you knew. I asked again what their names were and you gave two names of Greek gods and I laughed and we continued to speculate about what it was that they were doing. Was one running away from the other or were they playing a game? Was there ever a final embrace? You never answered. But the man who no one knew came and stood nearby watching us until I said I had to leave.

DIALOGUE:

X. You were wearing a black dress.

A. It cannot be.

X. With sequins down your back and along the neckline. And black gloves. Pearls.

A. I never.

X. You were here, and there were mirrors in the corridor. You were waiting. We were going out dancing. Or down to the lake for a stroll.

A. It is possible.

X. Of course it is possible, you told me in this very spot you would return this year.

A. I'm not sure. It is possible I've been here before.

X. I'm telling you, it is the case.

A. Perhaps it was a dream.

X. How do you explain the fact that I remember what you wore?

A. I think I remember our embrace by the lake.

X. There, you see.

A. But it is impossible. I must go.

X. You made a promise to return this year.

A. Leave me alone.

X. It is impossible.

A. I'm cold.

X. Let me help you put on your coat.

A. Until next year, then.

X. Will we meet again?

A. It is possible.

NARRATOR:

We walked through the corridors, endless and baroque, with mirrors along the hallways and ornate mantle pieces in every room. Each room is just like the rest, one bedroom is just like another and you were there suddenly and you turned and said to me you wanted me to come to Marienbad again next year and as it turns out you had remembered that I was there the year before and remembered the statues and that I had asked you what the names of the statues were and wondered whether maybe they were falling off a cliff or about to fall off a cliff and you laughed but you never answered you only described them – they could be us for all you knew. I asked again what their names were and you gave two names of Greek gods and I laughed and we continued to speculate about what it was that they were doing. Was one running away from the other or were they playing a game? Was there ever a final embrace? You never answered. But the man who no one knew came and stood nearby watching us until I said I had to leave.

DIALOGUE:

X. You were wearing a black dress.

A. It cannot be.

X. With sequins down your back and along the neckline. And black gloves. Pearls.

A. I never.

X. You were here, and there were mirrors in the corridor. You were waiting. We were going out dancing. Or down to the lake for a stroll.

A. It is possible.

X. Of course it is possible, you told me you would return this year.

A. I'm not sure. It is possible I've been here before.

X. I'm telling you, it is the case.

A. Perhaps it was a dream.

X. How do you explain the fact that I remember what you wore?

A. I think I remember our embrace by the lake.

X. There, you see.

A. But it is impossible. I must go.

X. You made a promise to me to return this year.

A. Leave me alone.

X. It is impossible.

A. I'm cold.

X. Let me help you put on your coat.

A. Until next year, then.

X. Will we meet again?

A. It is possible.

NARRATOR:

The woman put on her coat and gloves and walked down the corridor and up the stairs. The man walked to the lake and stood near the Greek statues that were about to fall off a cliff or lock in an embrace, one or the other. He looked at the lake and then at the endless symmetrical gardens, his eye following the narrowing point of perspective to the other side of the estate where the castle continued, where they had once met, where he could see the lights begin to dim, a time at dusk which slowly faded in his memory.

NOTES:

X = Man
A = Woman

GODARD

ALPHAVILLE

"Sometimes reality can be too complex to be conveyed by the spoken word."

Setting:
Alphaville, a city 150-200 years in the future.

Characters:
LEMMY CAUTION, Secret Agent 003, also known as
Ivan Johnson, a reporter from the Outer Countries
NATASCHA VON BRAUN, daughter of Professor
Von Braun, inhabitant of Alphaville
PROFESSOR VON BRAUN, advocate of logic and
technology
NARRATOR, also known as Alpha 60

She was a level 3 seductress. Her name: Natacha Von Braun.

NATACHA: I have orders to be at your service while you're
in Alphaville, Mr. Johnson.

*My name is Lemmy Caution, secret agent. I had only arrived
two hours earlier. I set my briefcase down and looked at her.*

LEMMY: Ordered by whom?

She has dark hair and big brown eyes like a cat.

NATACHA: The Authorities, of course.

I didn't like the sound of that, but her voice, her eyes kept me interested. Also on my guard.

NATACHA: Are you settled in now? We must hurry.

LEMMY: Why?

NATACHA: You mustn't ask 'why.' Besides, the festival you came to attend will be over soon.

LEMMY: All right. Let's go.

I kept my briefcase close to me even though several Level 2 attendants had offered to carry it ever since I had arrived.

NATACHA: Who are you, really?

LEMMY: Name's Ivan Johnson.

NATACHA: Monsieur Johnson, are you from the Outer Countries?

LEMMY: How'd you know that?

I looked at her cautiously. She seemed to think we had met before.

NATACHA: I don't know, Monsieur Johnson. I just guessed.

We took the spiral staircase down and went out onto the street.

It is dark. The lights of the city glow in rows like millions of fireflies, like hundreds of cats' eyes. Traffic passes by in circles, clocks tick, time passes; I don't know how much time, but everything slows down when I am with her. Something about her eyes and her manner of speaking get to me. She even walks differently than the others.

LEMMY: Has no one ever fallen in love with you?

NATACHA: Love? What is it?

You never understand anything about women, I tell myself, and what an idiot I am, asking her about love. Of course she hadn't any feelings for him. She had never learned what love was.

LEMMY: Don't you want me to proposition you? All the other girls around here seem to want that.

NATACHA: Thank you very much indeed, I'm fine, thank you.

LEMMY: Don't mention it.

Her smile reminds me of those vampire teeth you used to see at the cinema. She was a level 3 Seductress. Only doing her job. I needed to stop off at the Telecom Station to make a call so I tell her to go ahead and I will meet her at the festival.

AT THE TELECOM STATION:

ATTENDANT: Galaxy or local call?

LEMMY: Local please.

SOUND OF GUNFIRE
A Level 8 spy waiting in the phone booth for Lemmy slumps to the floor. Lemmy puts his gun back into his briefcase.

AT THE FESTIVAL
A room full of students, including Natacha, sit watching an educational documentary.

NARRATOR: 150-200 light years ahead, citizens have become slaves to probability. 150-200 years ago there were artists, painters, writers, poets; today, the humanities as we know them are close to extinction. Bibles have replaced dictionaries. Tenderness save for those who weep in private no longer exists. Words we once took for granted, such as natural light, organic produce, and love, have mostly disappeared.

ALPHA 60: 'NO ONE HAS EVER LIVED IN THE PAST, NO ONE WILL LIVE IN THE FUTURE. THE PRESENT IS THE ONLY FORM OF LIFE. IT IS A PASSION THAT NO FORCE CAN TAKE AWAY FROM US. TIME IS LIKE A CIRCLE, SPINNING INFINITELY.'

I was late to the festival, but I caught up with Natacha as she and the other festival-goers made their way out of the theater.

LEMMY: So, how was it?

NATACHA: This evening we learned that life and death exist all within the same circle.

Her voice is like that of a pretty sphinx. It echoes in my head, over and over, putting me in a trance. Suddenly, people are scurrying around us like ants, trying to get out of the building.

ON THE LOUDSPEAKER:
"Alpha 60 has declared war with the Outer Countries!"

NATACHA: What will you do?

LEMMY: I'll catch up with you later, Princess. I have to see a man about a riddle.

NATACHA: Are you sure you know what you are doing? Intelligent thinking and reasoning is forbidden in Alphaville.

LEMMY: Don't worry, sweetheart, I do this all the time.

ALPHA 60: LEMMY CAUTION, AGENT #003: YOU ARE A SECURITY THREAT TO ALPHAVILLE!

NATACHA: Did you hear that? They know you're not normal and they'll be coming for you soon! You'd better go.

LEMMY: I refuse to conform in order to become what you call 'normal.'

ALPHA 60: ORDINARY MEN ARE NOT WORTHY OF THE POSITION THEY HOLD IN THE WORLD. THOSE WHO RESIST ARE TO BE DESTROYED; THOSE THAT DO NOT CONFORM WILL BE EXECUTED. THERE IS A STRANGER IN OUR MIDST WHO MUST BE DESTROYED.

LEMMY: Last time I checked I was just an ordinary man, hmmmm.

ALPHA 60: BE ADVISED, THEY'VE WIPED OUT ALL SUPERIOR MUTANTS.

LEMMY: Listen here, Alpha 60, I have a secret. Something that never changes, by day or by night. The past represents its future, it goes forth in a straight line, yet it ends by coming full circle.

ALPHA 60: I DO NOT KNOW WHAT IT COULD BE.

LEMMY: I'm not going to tell you.

ALPHA 60: SEVERAL OF MY CIRCUITS ARE TRYING TO SOLVE YOUR RIDDLE. I'LL GET THERE.

LEMMY: If you solve it, you will destroy yourself, for you will have become my equal, my brother.

ALPHA 60: THOSE WHO HAVE NOT BEEN BORN DO NOT CRY AND HAVE NO REGRETS. IT IS THEREFORE LOGICAL TO SENTENCE YOU TO DEATH.

LEMMY: Go to hell!

ALPHA 60: IN MANY WAYS, YOUR ACTIONS AND YOUR THOUGHTS DIFFER FROM THE NORM, AGENT 003.

LEMMY: I hate to tell ya, but the people of Alphaville aren't normal. They're mutants!

ALPHA 60: MY JUDGEMENT IS JUST AND FOR THE GOOD OF ALL. DO YOU ACCEPT OUR PROPOSAL TO STAY AND CONFORM?

LEMMY: Like hell, I said, I will never betray the Outer Countries.

I suddenly felt dizzy and passed out. Must've been something in my drink. When I awoke I was in the office of Professor Von Braun.

PROFESSOR VON BRAUN: Stay with us, Mr. Caution. If you conform we'll put you in charge of your own galaxy. We're working on technology that is so far ahead it surpasses the Americans and the Russians. Their technologies will seem pathetic in comparison when we have finished. You can't go wrong…

I was still groggy from the drugs, but I wasn't gonna bite. What about the Koreans? Something tells me I was better off back home in the Outer Countries being abnormal. Mainly, I was thinking about Natacha; I needed to get back to her.

PROFESSOR VON BRAUN: I see now, you oppose my moral and supernatural sense of vocation with your simple physical and mental existence that is not easily controlled by technicians.

LEMMY: You're damn right I won't be controlled. People are still human beings, aren't they?

PROFESSOR VON BRAUN: Your ideas are strange, Mr. Caution. Back in the Age of Ideas your ideas would have been deemed sublime. Look at yourself. Men like you will soon be extinct. You will become worse than dead. You will become legendary for becoming a failure. Aren't you afraid of such a death?

LEMMY: Of course I'm afraid of death. But for a humble secret agent, it's become an everyday thing like whiskey. And I've been drinking all my life.

Lemmy kills the professor quickly with a bullet to his stomach. He returns to the hotel where Natacha is waiting.

NATACHA: I was ordered not to come, but I wanted to see you again.

She picks up his copy of The Capital of Pain he had forgotten to put inside his briefcase. She reads aloud the words that he had underlined.

NATACHA: "Are we near to, or far away from our conscience?" What does it mean, 'conscience'?

LEMMY: You don't know?

NATACHA: No one here knows what many of the old words mean anymore. I'm certain this word was in the bible yesterday, but now it's disappeared.

LEMMY: Princess, I hate to tell ya, that's not a bible, it's a dictionary!

NATACHA: Every day two words disappear and are replaced with new words, ugly words. Words I used to love, such as "Robin redbreast, autumn light, tenderness" no longer exist.

LEMMY: Sounds like you like poetry.

NATACHA [reading aloud]: 'Your eyes have returned from an arbitrary country where no one knows the meaning of a glance.' It's like dying and not dying.

LEMMY: Is that a secret message, Princess?

NATACHA: I'm starting to feel frightened since you've been here.

LEMMY: *Vous-avez peur de quoi?* What are you afraid of?

NATACHA: When I'm with you I'm afraid.

We drove together in my Ford Galaxy back to the festival — a series of lectures about the latest computer programs, process improvement, and environmental propaganda intermixed with advertising for the local Telecom company dominating the culture of Alphaville and its thought patterns. Afterwards, Natacha and I went back to the hotel for a drink. If I didn't know better I might have thought I was beginning to fall for her.

LEMMY: Where were you born?

NATACHA: In Alphaville.

LEMMY: Naaaah. I'd say you were born in Tokyo, the Land of the Rising Sun, or maybe it was Florence, where the sky is as blue as the south-seas, or perhaps it could have been New York, where in winter, Broadway glitters like snow on a fur coat. But not Alphaville.

NATACHA: You mock me. I tell you, my father was banished from Alphaville in 1964 for saying things like you just said. In Civil Control they still write and analyze such phrases, but no one normal understands them anymore.

LEMMY: In the Outer Countries, poets and artists still exist, sweetheart.

NATACHA: I'd like to go to the Outer Countries with you. Is that strange to say? Since I met you, I no longer feel normal."

LEMMY: No one in Alphaville is normal.

Natacha cast her eyes down at her drink....

LEMMY: Aren't you going to ask me why?

NATACHA: We aren't allowed to use the old words like 'how' and 'why.' Don't you understand? It's forbidden.

LEMMY: But you've already said 'why' to me at least once since we've been together.

NATACHA: When exactly did I say it?

LEMMY: When I said I was in love with you.

NATACHA: In love? What does that mean?

He retrieves a book of poetry from his briefcase and hands it to her.

LEMMY: Read this aloud. Read it to me.

NATACHA [reading aloud]: *"Your voice, your eyes, your hands, your lips, our silence. Light that fades away, light that comes back, one smile for the two of us...Out of my need for knowledge I watched night create day, while we remained unchanged. Oh beloved of all and beloved of one, your lips made a silent promise to be happy. Move away, away, says hatred, come closer, closer, says love. Our caresses lead us from our childhood, I am seeing a clearer image of the human form. Like lovers talking, the heat has but one mouth. Everything is haphazard, all words are spontaneous, feelings drift; men roam the city. Glances, words, and I love you. Everything moves, one need only advance to live. To go straight ahead towards all that you love. I was moving towards you. I was moving perpetually into the light."*

LEMMY: Well?

NATACHA: The words seem oddly familiar, but I'm still not sure what they mean.

She continues to read aloud, repeating the unfamiliar phrases from the book of poetry as if trying to remember: *"When you smile you become a part of me. The rays of your arms pierce the mist."*

A computerized voice over the loudspeaker pierces the stillness:

ALPHA 60: THE PRESENT IS TERRIFYING, BECAUSE IT IS IRREVERSIBLE, AND BECAUSE IT IS CAST IN IRON. THIS IS THE SUBSTANCE OF WHICH I AM MADE.

NATACHA: *"Time is a river that carries me along. But I am Time. It is a tiger tearing me apart. But I am a tiger."*

LEMMY: Look at us. There is your answer. We are happiness, and that's where we are heading. Unfortunately for us, the world is real.

ALPHA 60: AND ME, UNFORTUNATELY FOR ME, I AM ME, ALPHA 60.

There is a powerful explosion and the ceiling collapses and streams of natural light begin flooding in to the building, causing all the inhabitants to scurry out of their rooms and offices, and into the corridors, like ants. People struggle to breathe, pulling against gravity as if there was a lack of air, clinging to the walls, lining the corridors like dying flies in a nuclear blast, like zombies.

Natacha struggles against the urgency to run, but is unable to stay upright without using the walls as support. The lack of artificial light and natural air is debilitating as her body is unaccustomed to fresh air and sunlight. She stumbles, pulling herself along the corridor with Lemmy holding her arm.

LEMMY: Natacha, think of the word 'love,' it will keep you upright.

Natacha and I left Alphaville at 11:05pm Oceanic time, driving all night through intersidereal space. We would be back home to the Outer Countries by the next day. I tried to remind her to not look behind her. Never look back. Alphaville was self-destructing.

NATACHA: Do you think they're all dead?

LEMMY: Some may recover eventually, but I'm not taking any chances.

NATACHA: You're looking at me oddly, as if you're waiting for me to say something. I don't know what to say; I don't know the words. Help me.

LEMMY: Impossible, Princess. You have to get there yourself. If you can't remember the words, then you're as lost as the dead souls of Alphaville.

Natacha casts her eyes straight ahead and watches the road for several minutes.

NATACHA (whispering): Je vous aime. I love you.

FIN

MARKER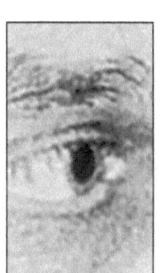

SANS SOLEIL (SUNLESS)

"Because I know that time is always time and place is always and only place..."
– T.S. Eliot, *Ash Wednesday* (beginning of *Sans Soleil*)

[NARRATOR]

"The first image he sent me was an image of three children on a road in Iceland in 1965. He said that for him, it was the image of happiness, and also that he had tried several times to link it to other images, but it never worked. One day I'll have to put it at the beginning of a film with a long black leader. If they don't see happiness in the film, at least they'll see the black."

He wrote...

"I've been 'round the world several times, and now only banality still interests me. On this trip, I've tracked it with the relentlessness of a bounty hunter."

He appreciated the fragility of those banal moments, and likened them somehow to "the spiral of time" as expressed in Hitchcock's *Vertigo*. He said that only one film had been capable of portraying impossible memory, insane memory... Alfred Hitchcock's *Vertigo*, in which Madelaine's (Kim Novak's) hair is a spiral.

He said it was *impossible to live with memory* without

falsifying it. He wanted to "repair the web of time where it had been broken."

He wrote me that in the suburbs of Tokyo there is a temple consecrated to cats. I wish I could convey the simplicity of that temple and the visitors to it, who were paying homage to the spirit of their deceased beloved pets.

"In that moment in time," he wrote, "poetry will be made by everyone, and there will be emus in the zone."

He was questioning his own memory, at that point, his own happiness. He was questioning the interpretation of memory. He said that as soon as you intellectualize it, it becomes something else.

Memory is a sense. A memory of your own is not expressed in words: it's a visualization in our mind's eye. Not a photograph; A photograph is not the same. Feelings overwhelm the reality of that memory.

[FLASHBACK]

She took a sketchbook and a camera with her everywhere, wanting to capture and record every moment. To her all things were alive and moments were too precious to be forgotten. She wanted him to know. She would send photos from her phone along with text messages, describing what she saw. Sometimes she photographed the sea, the cliffs where she hiked – and would send photos of the native plants and herbs bending in the wind. Other times she would sketch and describe the landscapes or cityscapes: A café, the city lights, her pets, a country church, a meadow. She felt the need to hold on to time. But how could she remember what it felt like to hold him, make love to him, hold his hand? And so, she wrote him to keep his spirit with her, even if his responses vacillated or were vague, and she couldn't keep specific memories of him as close as she would have liked. She wrote and travelled, doing as she pleased, but always sent the recorded moments to him.

It was hard to tell where her journey began and where it ended, because she sometimes felt she was repeating the same sentences, the same words and images. She noted pigeons, for example, how they flocked together in the square. People would throw seed and the pigeons would immediately flock, oblivious to their surroundings. They'd only bob their heads and wings and disperse in a flutter when a car or a running child passed through the square. Otherwise, they pecked and bobbed endlessly. She photographed them, and the statues on which they had left their white splatter. Then she would move on, and there were always more pigeons. And so, she wrote him.

She took the train watching the people sitting, standing, talking, reading, eating, crying, playing music, singing, and she would try to think of someone else with whom she might share her observations. But the train would stop, and the people or person in question would get off, and the train would move again, and the moment would be over. She recorded these moments, as if she were dreaming them.

The green and brown landscape would pass by, and time would flutter in the flicker of windows, in the light passing, through tunnel after tunnel. She got off the train once it stopped and she would stand in a new place and take in the sights. When she walked through the villages and saw people who were hungry and thirsty she would give them money, then take their picture or sketch them. She travelled this way, and when she stopped to rest she often couldn't stop the images and memories from seeping in at night before sleep.

She couldn't remember where they'd been together last and where she'd been on her own. Each place she visited remained in her memory as one she'd visited with him, so it didn't matter, except when she tried to make chronological sense of her sketchbooks and journals. Eventually, she would write him, and send him an image or a text and he would remember. And the moments continued as she travelled.

TRUFFAUT

*I have always preferred the
reflection of the life to life itself.*

EXT. FILM SET – DAY

A bustling outdoor movie set, somewhere on the French Riviera. A crowded city street scene is in progress, traffic and pedestrians in syncronized motion. FRANCOIS TRUFFAUT is directing this film within a film. He is seated on a platform atop a scaffold.

Two SPECTATORS stand among a small crowd of onlookers in a taped-off area.

                    SPECTATOR #1
        Cool, we get to watch a film being filmed!

                    SPECTATOR #2
        It's a film about filmmaking.

                    SPECTATOR #1
        What's the film called?

                    SPECTATOR #2
        The film, or the film within the film?

                    SPECTATOR #1
        I meant the film within the film.

                    SPECTATOR #2
        Oh, that film is called *Je Vous Présente
        Paméla. Meet Pamela*, also referred to as *I
        want you to meet Pamela*.

SPECTATOR #1
And what is the title of the film?

SPECTATOR #2
This film? You'd have to ask the author. If you mean, the film being filmed, it's *La Nuit Américaine,* or *Day for Night*.

SPECTATOR #1
What does the title signify?

SPECTATOR #2
It is named after the filmmaking process referred to in French as *la nuit américaine* "American night," whereby sequences filmed outdoors in daylight are shot using film stock balanced for tungsten—indoor light— and underexposed or adjusted during post production to appear as if they are taking place at night. In English, the technique is called *day for night* and is the film's English title.

SPECTATOR #1
What a clever title!

ON ALPHONSE, the film's handsome, dark-haired leading man as he emerges from the subway stairs onto the bustling avenue. WE FOLLOW HIM as he crosses the street.

DIRECTOR
Cut!

(to the crew)
The timing is off.

He climbs down and crosses to Alphonse.

DIRECTOR
Are you on a Sunday stroll here, Alphonse?
You're supposed to be in a hurry, remember?
You're late. Let's try and get the lead out this
time.

He returns to his platform, picks up a megaphone.

DIRECTOR
OK, everybody back on your marks, we're
taking it from the top. Five seconds.

Everone takes their positions.

DIRECTOR
(into megaphone)
Lights...camera...ACTION..sound!

A car MOVES into frame and passes two old ladies
waiting for a bus in the background. Alphonse walks
briskly out of the subway and crosses the street.

CLOSE ON A MAN with a distinct angular face. He
wears thick, black-rimmed sunglasses and a tweed
jacket. He stares directly into the camera, silently
smoking a cigarette.

SPECTATOR #1 (VOICEOVER)
How strange to have a man suddenly appear
out of nowhere!

SPECATOR #2 (VOICEOVER)
Smoking a cigarette, too. It's called a nonse-
quiteur. It's a disruption of the scene.

SPECTATOR #1 (VOICEOVER)
It certainly isn't a smooth transition. Who is
the man, anyway?

SPECTATOR #2 (VOICEOVER)
It's Godard. I've been waiting to meet him my
whole life!

DISSOLVE TO:

EXT. FILM SET - LATER

ON GODARD and TRUFFAUT as they stand arguing at
the base of the scaffolding.

GODARD
I cannot believe you are allowing her to use
this film. It is outrageous!

TRUFFAUT
What in the world do you mean, Godard?

GODARD
La Nuit Americaine, *Day for Night*, of course. It

is a huge farce, a tremendous lie!

PULL BACK to include two film fans standing in the rear spectator area

TRUFFAUT FAN
What is that man doing here? He is such an elitist intellectual snob.

GODARD FAN
Godard is brilliant; he understands the true meaning of film-making: a true anarchist, unlike your commercial sell-out, Truffaut.

CLOSE ON Truffaut and Godard.

TRUFFAUT
Jean Luc, keep your angular face and dark sunglasses out of this. If she wants to include *Day for Night*, she includes it. Perhaps she sees the importance of using a film that was not only made in the seventies (after the French New Wave had run its course), but also a film about the love of film-making and the dying art of studio-made films; a film that won the academy award for Best Foreign Languge Film in 1974, along with many other awards; a film that addresses the theme of whether or not films are more important than life and for those who make them, its many allusions both to film-making and to movies themselves; a film which deliberately invites viewers to recognize

the artificiality of cinema – particularly the kind of American-style studio film, with its reliance on effects like day-for-night, that *Je Vous Présente Paméla* exemplifies; in summary, she is referencing a poignant film here.

GODARD
No one else is going to tell you the truth, so I will: The film is a lie. A piece of junk!

TRUFFAUT
You are just jealous because I got to work with big stars and my movie was a huge commercial success whereas your films remained relatively unknown!

GODARD
You are nothing but a bourgeois sell-out! Ms. Wilson could have used *400 Blows*, *Shoot the Piano Player*, *Jules et Jim*, or even *Fahrenheit 451*, for goodness sake!

TRUFFAUT
I'm the director here, and you're not in this scene, Godard. You there! What happened? You were supposed to keep the area clear while we shot this scene!

The producer crosses over to Truffaut.

PRODUCER
Hey, François! The press wants to interview

the actors. Can we spare a couple?

SCRIPT GIRL
Look here, we're behind schedule,
François. Those two are needed over in make-
up, pronto.

PROP BOY
Monsieur Truffaut! Is this the correct kind of
gun you want for the shooting scene? Do you
prefer this gun, or that gun?

TRUFFAUT
That one.

REPORTER
I'm from the newspaper Nice-Matin, could we
have a word, please?

TRUFFAUT
Give me a moment, please.

STUNT MANAGER
We will need to substitute the Austin Martin
for the Citroën in the car chase scene. We
found a blue one and a green one. Which
do you want?

TRUFFAUT
(sighs; looks at the reader)
What is a director? Someone who is asked questions

about everything. Sometimes he knows the answers, sometimes he doesn't. [To the Stunt Manager] I prefer the blue!

PRODUCER
The Americans want this finished in seven weeks! Can we do it, Truffaut?

SCRIPT GIRL
We can do it, François. We'll make it happen. If Séverine would stop drinking and remember her lines, that is.

SÉVERINE
I'm sorry, I'm trying my best! [starts crying] I can't seem to remember my lines anymore.

SCRIPT GIRL
[to reader]
She's so *old* now, no wonder.

TRUFFAUT
Don't worry, Séverine. Jaqueline! Where is Jaqueline? Where is my lead actress, where is my Pamela?

SCRIPT GIRL
She's in her room, speaking to Alphonse. He's down in the dumps because Liliane left him for the stunt driver.

TRUFFAUT
We need them both in this scene!

SCRIPT GIRL
I told you, Alphonse is extremely distraught
and is threatening not to finish the film!

TRUFFAUT
Good god, I knew Liliane was going to cause
trouble...Let's call it a day, everyone. We'll
begin again tomorrow morning.

INT. THE SET — EARLY MORNING

TRUFFAUT
Good morning, everyone! We must proceed
quickly, so listen carefully: I want no sentimen-
tality in this scene, do you understand? Just
play it straight, cold. Let's start with the love
scene.

CUT TO:

INT. APARTMENT — NIGHT

JAQUELINE and ALPHONSE'S FATHER are sitting in a
dimly lit kitchen.

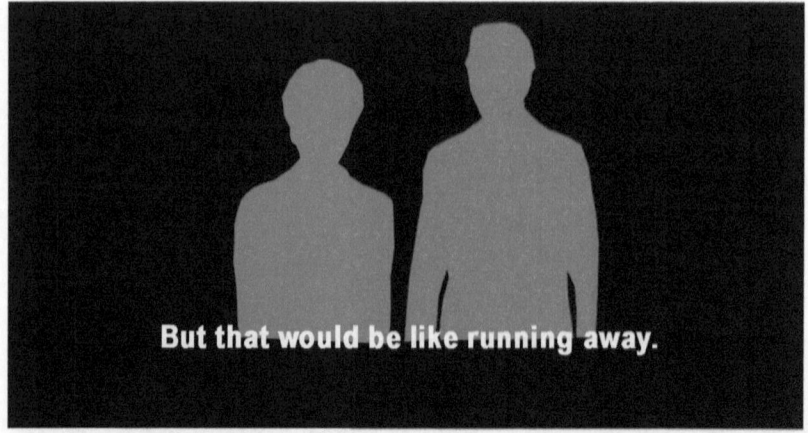

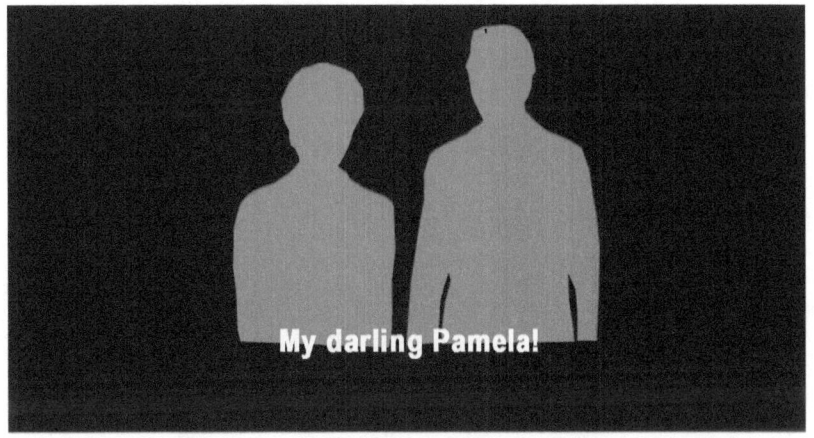

TRUFFAUT

Cut! The doctor has forgotten his toupee!
What's that cat doing here?! Script Girl!
(to reader)
Shooting a movie is something like a stage-
coach ride in the Old West. At first you are
just hoping for a nice trip. Soon, problems
start coming at you from all sides and you
only hope to reach your destination!

GODARD

What kind of melodromatic slop is this?

TRUFFAUT

Actually, with only seven weeks to go, I hope
to finish the film, period.

SPECTATOR #1 (VOICEOVER)

Poor Alphonse! His wife is in love with his
own father!

SPECTATOR #2 (VOICEOVER)
Poor Séverine, her husband can no longer
stand to look at her, she is so old and con-
fused.

The filming continues late into the night.

DISSOLVE TO:

INT. TRUFFAUT'S BEDROOM – NIGHT

Truffaut is in bed, tossing and turning, haunted by
scenes from his childhood and DIALOGUES from
throughout the day.

In his mind he sees a FLASHING neon sign: "CINEMA."

DISSOLVE TO:

EXT. THE SET – NEXT MORNING

TRUFFAUT stands at a kiosk, sipping coffee and checking checking the script. The SCRIPT GIRL
approaches.

TRUFFAUT
Where is Alphonse? He's in the next scene
with Jaqueline!

SCRIPT GIRL
He has locked himself in his room and won't
come out. I told you, Liliane left him abruptly for

the stunt man after Alphonse proposed to her.

CUT TO:

INT. HOTEL – MOMENTS LATER

We follow TRUFFAUT as he walks briskly through the hotel corridor. He stops at room #18 and knocks sharply on the door.

TRUFFAUT
Alphonse! Open this door at once!

A long beat. The door opens slowly and Alphonse steps into the corridor. He is barefoot, wearing a knee-length white night shirt.

ALPHONSE
I need money to go to a whorehouse.

TRUFFAUT
Go back in your room, Alphonse, and study your lines for tomorrow.

ALPHONSE
I'm quitting the film, I won't continue!

TRUFFAUT
Alphonse, no one's private life runs smoothly. That only happens in films. No traffic jams, no dead periods. Movies speed along like trains – like trains in the night. People like you and I are

only happy when we are in our work. Our lives are illusions. We are all actors in some kind of drama. Directors can play God, but ultimately, we are all actors in some kind of illusion that is so-called life.

ALPHONSE
I am leaving and not finishing the film. I cannot concentrate. I am a physical wreck!

SCRIPT GIRL
Is there anyone who can convince you to stay?

ALPHONSE
I will only speak to Jaqueline!

He steps back into his room – slams the door.

INT. HOTEL CORRIDOR – A FEW MINUTES LATER

CLOSE ON
Jacqueline as she knocks on the door.

JAQUELINE
Alphonse, I know how hurt you are. But I still think Liliane loves you. You're being selfish, too. You know how difficult it is for an outsider to live with an actor.

ALPHONSE (OFF SCREEN)
OK, but to leave without saying goodbye and

to leave with just anyone! Some Brit stunt-
man!

                    JAQUELINE
Hey, watch it! I'm British, too. Please open the
door now.

The door opens very slowly, just enough for Jaqueline to
slip inside.

INT. ALPHONSE'S ROOM – CONTINUOUS

                    JAQUELINE
I'm sure it will be over soon between them.
You know how impulsive Liliane is. These
affairs never last long. She'll be back in two
weeks.

                    ALPHONSE
Maybe you are right. Anyway, my love affairs
have always ended badly.

                    JAQUELINE
Besides, I'm sure François is wrong. Life is
more important than films.

                    ALPHONSE
You've helped me make up my mind and
I'm going now. Thank you for everything.

                    JAQUELINE
Don't be a fool. Stay here and finish the film.

CUT TO:

GODARD frowning.

GODARD
Don't tell me: in the next scene they sleep together.

DISSOLVE TO:

INT. HOTEL BEDROOM – NEXT MORNING

JAQUELINE and ALPHONSE in bed. She wakes, glances over at Alphonse who is snoring. She smiles, slips out of bed and sneaks out of the room.

SPECTATOR #1 (VOICEOVER)
I'm not sure that was such a good idea. Isn't Jaqueline married?

SPECTATOR #2 (VOICEOVER)
Yes, but these things happen on a film set.

CUT TO:

GODARD
Utter rubbish!

DISSOLVE TO:

INT. LA PISCINE RESTAURANT - NIGHT

The entire cast and crew are gathered together for Séverine's farewell dinner.

PRODUCER
A toast! A toast to Séverine, what a pro she has been!

SCRIPT GIRL
(raising her glass)
Here's to you, my dear!

TRUFFAUT
 Let's have Alphonse buy us another round, eh?! Where is he, anyway?

SÉVERINE
Goodbye everyone! It has been amazing working with you all! Imagine: We meet, we work together, we love each other, and then 'poof!' it's over! I must go now. I will bid you adieu, until we meet again!

FADE TO BLACK

BERGMAN

PERSONA

Two slim cylindrical film bulbs merge at the beginning of the film, letting off a bright white flash! Primitive cartoons and goofy music plays. A film reel clicks and turns. A close-up of an eye. A sheep in a field. Two elegant hands curling and twisting entwined in a dance...a bright white screen. A nail is being pounded into a (crucified) hand. An insect. Dramatic music. A quiet forest. An old gate. Dirty snow. A dead woman sleeping in an empty room. A dead boy on a gurney. A dead man sleeping. A pair of feet. A telephone ringing. Water dripping. A boy under the sheet on the gurney turns away from the camera as if he wants to go back to sleep. The sheet doesn't cover him. He gets up, turns to the camera, puts on his glasses. Reads a book. Looks at the camera a bit. Sits up, puts his hand on the lens over the image of a woman. Over her face, her mouth, her eyes. Liv Ullman? The music becomes more and more dramatic, the credits flash, the boy, a monk, the natural world, a white screen, the boy, Liv's face, old movies...The nurse comes in and speaks to Liv, who is having a conversation with Ingmar...

INGMAR: Why aren't you speaking? Must you insist on continuing to inhabit your role as Elisabet Vogler in *Persona*?

LIV: If that were the case, then you would be playing the role of Alma, my nurse. Besides, I thought you might enjoy doing most of the talking.

INGMAR: Very amusing.

Water drips, a xylophone plunks a cacophonous tune, trees, rocks, wind chimes, the xylophone again, timpani drums rumbling...

LIV: In *Persona*, my character (an actress) fell silent after a performance of Electra one night. She spoke her last line, looked around as if in surprise, and didn't speak a word for the next several months. She didn't go to rehearsal the next day, and wouldn't speak to anyone. Doctors diagnosed her as healthy mentally and physically but not emotionally. Is this what you think of me?

INGMAR: I think it shows great mental strength to decide not to speak. I am not judging you, in any case. I think Alma (your nurse) was right when she was concerned about not being mature enough to handle your mind games.

LIV: *My* mind games? You created the character of Elisabet Vogler. You are the one who is inside her head, not me. I was just playing the role as you asked me to play it, alongside Bibi Anderson, your former lover, by the way.

INGMAR: The two of you were wonderful. Looked so much alike in your black sunglasses, bathing suits and big hats...

LIV: During the five years we lived together with our daughter, I always did as you asked, stayed out of the way, cooked and took care of you; our home became a prison when you wouldn't let me out of your sight. Despite our great love, it was you controlling me. Always.

INGMAR: You were an impressionable young girl who was smitten, what can I say?

LIV: I was so happy for a long time. Especially in the beginning. Despite the fact that you were married five times (never to me, of course) and had nine children. How many films did we make together?

INGMAR: Twelve.

LIV: How many years did we know each other?

INGMAR: Forty years altogether. You were always my muse.

LIV: In all that time, critics and analysts are still trying to decipher your films, especially *Persona*.

INGMAR: At some time or other, I said that *Persona* saved my life—that is no exaggeration. If I had not found the strength to make that film, I would probably have been all washed up. One significant point: for the first time I didn't care in the least whether the result would be a commercial success...

LIV: You were recovering from pneumonia when you wrote it, I remember. You wrote about it afterward.

INGMAR: I had gone as far as I could go, I felt, after I had written *Persona*. And that is because I had been working in total freedom, I touched wordless secrets that only the cinema can discover...

LIV: It was shot on the island of Fårö in summer. We had beautiful weather.

INGMAR: My beautiful muse.

LIV: I don't think you really understood me. I was playing a role. I was so desperate sometimes.

INGMAR: But I do. I understand 'that hopeless dream of being. Not seeming to be, but being. Conscious and awake at every moment. At the same time the chasm between what you are to others and what you are to yourself. The feeling of vertigo and the constant conscious hope of being unmasked. To be seen through, cut down, perhaps even annihilated… Every tone of voice a lie, every gesture, a falsehood. Every smile, a grimace. Commit suicide? No, too nasty. One doesn't do things like that…But you can refuse to move or talk. Then at least you're not lying. You can cut yourself off, close yourself off then you needn't play any roles, wear any masks, or make any false gestures.

LIV: But reality plays nasty tricks on you. Your hiding place isn't watertight. Life oozes in from all sides. You're forced to react. No one asks whether it's genuine or not, whether you're lying or telling the truth…

INGMAR: Questions like that only matter in the theatre, and hardly even there. I understand you and admire you. I think you should play this part until it's played out…until it's no longer interesting. Then you can drop it just as you eventually drop all your other roles…'

LIV: That's not fair. You're describing my character, not me. I think it actually describes more how *you* feel rather than me.

INGMAR: Perhaps I write myself into your character's lines.

LIV: Perhaps I've absorbed everything you've taught me during the past forty years.

INGMAR: Tell me, I want to hear what you've absorbed. I want to hear your secrets.

LIV: Do you want to hear about my lovers? You've heard all my stories. Tell me about your childhood.

INGMAR: You already know about all of it. Tell me.

LIV: Only if it will put the subject to rest. I remember it all like one long torment. I was terribly in love and it went on for five years. Then he got tired of it. There were long periods of agony...Your teaching me how to smoke reminded me. He smoked constantly...It all seems unreal. In some strange way it was never quite real. I don't know how to explain it. I suppose I was unreal to him. But my pain was real, that's for sure. In hind-sight, it all seems so dreary. A real dime-store novel. Even the things we said to each other. But that was all part of it in some nasty way, as if it was meant to be that way... You're the first person who has ever listened to me and I've never felt this way in my whole life... (takes a sip of wine)... But don't let me go on babbling this way... You asked me to tell you... Am I being silly?

[They talk all night, finishing the wine]

INGMAR: You're right. I've heard your stories before.

LIV: Go to bed, or you'll fall asleep here at the table.

INGMAR: No, I must go to bed, or I'll fall asleep at the table, and that would be rather uncomfortable.

LIV: Good night.

INGMAR: Embrace me.

LIV: Become me.

INGMAR: Did you speak to me last night?

LIV: Were you in my room last night?

INGMAR: No.

LIV: No.

INGMAR: It is raining. Pour the coffee.

LIV: Would you like a cigarette?

WELLES

TOUCH OF EVIL

"People moving out, people moving in, why?, because of the color of their skin. Run, run, run, but you just can't hide…"

— The Temptations

The scene opens with a close up of a hand turning the dial of an egg-timer as Henry Mancini-jazzy bongo drums speed up into a frenzied, snappy staccato.

CLOSE-UP: a self-made bomb (the timer is attached to a few curly wires, attached to a bundle of dynamite) which is then placed furtively by the unidentified hand into the trunk of a large, white American 1950s era car.

A smartly dressed MAN and A WOMAN (Heston and Leigh) cross the street at a steady clip, arm in arm, in sync with the music. They weave in and out of the shadows and back into the light again. They cross the street, headed towards the border crossing.

A COUPLE laughing, dressed for a night on the town get in the big white car and begin driving SLOWLY up the lively, seedy street of Los Robles, a Mexican-American border town, headed home.

"People moving out, people moving in, why, because of the color of their skin.

Run, run, run, but you just can't hide..."

The couple on foot reaches the border first, and exchange a few words with the border patrol officer as they are about to cross over.

The car with the jolly couple behind in the American car had just caught up to them, when the bomb EXPLODES.

Henry Mancini bongo DRUMS BEAT FASTER and HORNS SCREAM.

MARLENE DIETRICH: Of all things, the egg timer attached to the homemade bomb was the last thing I would have expected as an opener for the first scene. But we were shooting a low budget movie. A film that was shot in 38 days. No wonder it had to be a low-budget bomb. This was a noir film. The last of the noir films, at least, it was made at the end of the original film noir period. This was a film made with hand-held cameras, lots of distorted wide angles, very little light, subtle camera moves, shadows cast across low lit buildings, gritty streets; a film that became famous for its style, sound, edits; a story told with "startling realism."

My character, Tania, is an exotic gypsy who runs a brothel on the seedy side of town. I was happy to play the part because I had always been a little in love with Orson. No matter that I only appear in about three or four scenes. I am a huge screen presence and I look good in close ups. Besides, I'm always on his mind throughout the film. I know that. I'm the one he comes to see when he's lonely, scared, and desperate, out of control. After he kills Papa Grandi and comes to see me he asks me to talk to him, tell him his future. I tell him:

"Listen, Quinlan, you ain't got no future."

"Why?" he says...

"You're a mess, honey. You oughta lay off the candy bars, I hardly recognized you." It had been a million years since I'd seen him, since his wife had been killed and the killer ran free.

"It's either the candy bars or the booze," he says.

He's wearing a fat-suit for the Quinlin character in this film. It might not be an entire fat-suit, but he's definitely padded up to make himself look even more evil. He plays a corrupt detective, but he wasn't that way when our characters first met. When we were both young he used to come to my place once in a while. Ok, he came over all the time. Middle of the night. All hours of the night. Didn't matter if I had other customers, he would wait.

"You got any of that chili you used to make?" he says. "I wish it was your chili I was getting fat on."

"You'd better be careful," I tell him. "It may be too hot for you."

He leaves again, and the next time I see him he's dead, or at least dying. Shot by his partner.

The thing about Orson is he is a genius director. I don't know what else to say. I guess he picked me to tell this story because I could appreciate his genius. He wanted me to write about it, to document the film in some way.

"What should I write about?" I asked him. What could I say that hadn't already been said before about this genius B-movie?

"Approach it like a painter capturing the heart of noir," he says. "Think shapes, geometry, shadows, sharp angles, serrated dialogue."

MARLENE: Are those some of your best filmmaking techniques?

ORSON: Oh, there are a million different types of shots: the pedestal shot, the low angle shot, the low lighting, the deep focus, deep shadows, highlighted sounds…

MARLENE: Breaking glass, the microphone close-up, distortion of dialogue…

ORSON: The choreography of the camera and the talent to maximize the effect…

MARLENE: One of my favorite scenes is the first shot of the strip club when Zsa Zsa comes walking down the steps and you cut to a piece of trash blowing across the screen. And what about the light bulb scene with Janet Leigh when the Grandi boy is watching her from across the street?

ORSON: Thanks, honey. It means a lot.

MARLENE: I'll leave it to the author to write about the film. I don't know what else to say.

ORSON: Yeah, let the unidentified narrator work it out.

UNIDENTIFIED NARRATOR(S):

—*Touch of Evil*? What is it about?
—Do you mean 'what is evil about this film?'
—I mean what is your interpretation of evil?
—Orson Welles' character Quinlin is evil personified.
—Is he all bad?
—It depends.
—On what?
—On whether you believe that evil can only exist in revenge-seeking, power-hungry corrupt cops.
—I don't think Quinlan was power-hungry. Not at first. But he was revenge-seeking. His wife was killed by a killer that got away. Where is the justice in that?
—Who's talking about *justice*?
—I was referring to it.
—Were you making the point that this film contains elements of good versus evil, justice versus corruption?
—Who has the right to take the law into one's own hands?
—Makes me think about Agatha Christie themes...
—Or Dostoyevski or Kafka? How about Trump?
—That's a scary thought. Can one compare Trump to Quinlin?
—Trump is a thinner, more glamorous version of Quinlin.
—Did Quinlin call evil by its own name?
—That was more something Vargas would have done. He

would have called a white supremacist a white supremacist.
—Vargas was a good guy?
—Charleton Heston is always a 'good' guy, even if he is a Republican.
—I thought you weren't going to get into politics.
—In this case, in light of the Charlottesville protests I am making an exception.
—Wasn't there a bomb at the beginning of *Touch of Evil*?
—A hand-made bomb. Looked like an egg-timer attached to a bunch of wires strapped to a small bundle of dynamite.
—When was the last time you thought about bombs?
—Recently. Frequently. Often.
—Terrorism?
—Nice, Paris, Munich, London, Barcelona…when will it end?
—Speaking of bombs, can we talk about bombshells? This film is full of them.
—Yes, but the bombshell characters in this film (Marlene Dietrich, Janet Leigh, Zsa Zsa Gabor) are not femme fatales as in most noir films.
—Strange because this film is hyper-noir.
—So why aren't you riffing off of it?
—I'm thinking about evil more than noir.
—I can understand that.
—Racism, corruption, greed. Drugs. Murder. A lot of evil going on.
—Which leads me back to my original question. Can evil exist without good?
—In Quinlin's case, he has Tania, who isn't all that good herself.
—Tania played by Marlene Dietriech.

—She loved Quinlin.

—Despite the fact that he was crooked. Put away many an innocent man. Killed a man himself, in front of a drugged and hallicinating Janet Leigh.

—You mean Grandi? Maybe that act of evil was actually an act of *good* because it helped Janet Leigh.

—She wasn't too happy when she woke up and saw Grandi flung across her bedpost, eyes bulging out of his head staring at her.

—I don't imagine so. Still. Grandi was trying to get Vargas. At least, he tried to get at him through his wife.

—Did he get to her in the end?

—Did Grandi get Susie? There was an implied rape scene, imposed on Susie by the Vargas gang, but seems that Susie came out of it unscathed.

—Chuck Heston got to do a great enragement scene where the veins in his throat bulged out and he smashed up an entire bar-room, shouting 'MY WIFE! WHAT HAVE YOU DONE WITH MY WIFE?!'

—Grandi was definitely evil for doing that to Susie.

—Was Orson justified in killing him, then?

—It's a dog-eat-dog world in Paso Robles.

—Kind of like the Wild West.

—And what about the Mexican kid who was framed? Did he really plant the bomb in the trunk of that car?

—Could be. Maybe he did, maybe he didn't.

—And what about Quinlan's partner, Menzies? He finally did the right thing by letting Vargas set Quinlan up, right?

—Menzies finally realized the man he had idolized all that time was corrupt. It's a good thing Marlene (Tania) was there to say goodbye in the end.

—Yeah, lucky for the audience she was in the final scene and got to say a few last words about Quinlan.

—What was it she said?

—"He was some kind of man."

—Menzies asks her: "Aren't you going to say anything else about him?"

—"What does it matter what you say about people?" she says.

—"So long, Tania."

—"Adios."

ERSHADI

TASTE OF CHERRY

I was to interview Homayoun Ershadi (Mr. Badii) after the filming had concluded. I wasn't sure how he would respond to being interviewed so soon after the grave scene, but I took a chance and walked up to him and offered him a cigarette. He was gracious and accepted, seeming to understand I wasn't your everyday journalist. He even lit my Dunhill Red as I began asking questions:

CW: I hope you like this brand; I noticed you lit one of yours and gave it away to Mr. Kiarostami. Why did you do that?

HE: We have been friends a long time. I knew he wanted a smoke, and he had a lot on his mind with the conclusion of the filming so I gave it to him. It was intended to be a gesture of friendship.

CW: The shot in which you give him the cigarette was not edited out in the last, controversial scene of the film. Was it intentionally included?

HE: Yes. Mr. Kiarostami wanted the familiarity between us shown. He wanted the audience to get a sense of real life continuing even as the film, and perhaps my character's life, concluded.

CW: Can you tell me more about that? Are we, the audience meant to believe that your character really committed suicide (a concept that is taboo in Iran), or is another meaning to be interpreted? Is Mr. K condoning suicide?

HE: I would have to say it is up to the individual to decide. For each of us there may be a different ending to Mr. Badii's story. Mr. K wanted to demonstrate that the individual's outlook on life, and ultimately the degree to which he finds happiness, is not only a matter of what cultural values impose upon us; we also have a choice. It is rather a matter of how we respond to the questions that life throws at us. This is also demonstrated by Mr. K's use of non-professionals as actors. In many cases, scenes were shot with the director asking the non-actors questions, and filming their responses, often unrehearsed. In doing so, Mr. K captures 'real life' reactions to the topic of suicide from various cultural perspectives. As far as cultural taboos, certainly Mr. K wanted to address them.

CW: You mentioned individual choice. What would you say is the choice Mr. K would have us make?

HE: Well, first of all, as far as the film is concerned, we must decide what Mr. Badii's fate was, ultimately. Did he kill himself or not? On the one hand, he appears to have made all the preparations in order to commit suicide. On the other, the preparations he makes are not in keeping with a man who is entirely indifferent to life. He worries about the details of his death, even going so far as to return to the taxidermist to request that he throw two stones on him to make sure he is dead. It is through Mr. Badii's actions that we begin to see that he does have a choice. He prepares for death, yes. He imagines what it will be like to be buried alive, even as he sits and lets the dust and noise of the heavy machinery and bulldozers envelop his senses. When we see shots of the mounds of dirt and earth being bulldozed in the construction sites we imagine the sense of suffocation Badii must feel. But is the suffocation he experiences in life worse than what he would feel were he to be buried alive? That is his choice, ultimately. And the director lets the audience make that choice as well. Which is better? It may also be that the concept of suffocation is used as a metaphor for being silenced. Do you see what I mean?

CW: Yes. Yet your character seems to hesitate a bit about committing suicide the farther he drives along. There seem to be various "red herrings" if you will, designed to lead the audience into believing Badii has not lost all hope. I.e.: the innocence of playing children in the beginning, the fork in the road Badii encounters with Mr. Bagheri after his mulberry story, the helpfulness of the peasants when his car turns over, the flocks of birds, the soaring plane overhead in the cloudless sky, the beautiful sunset he experiences on the bench overlooking the city, and then the rain storm; aren't these all cinematographic tricks meant to lead the audience into believing that in the end Badii will change his mind and choose life instead of death?

HE: These "red herrings" as you call them; I believe they are all intended to make us think.

CW: Make us think about what, exactly?

HE: The cycles in Life. Each of us has certainly experienced

CARLA M. WILSON

moments of happiness, followed by periods of grief or despair. These moments may not be as extreme as artists would indicate; nevertheless, cycles exist. Happiness and despair go hand in hand. We cannot have one without the other. Isn't it true that we may enjoy the taste of life's delicious fruit more when we experience great sadness?

CW: Yes, I suppose you're right. So what did Mr. K want his audience to feel, ultimately? Would he want us to be sympathetic with Mr. Badii and his choice?

HE: I do not believe that he would want to influence the audience one way or the other, emotionally. He wanted to keep emotions at a distance, therefore we do not find out very much about Badii's character and his motivation for committing suicide. It does not matter, ultimately, what has driven him to despair. The director gives us clues: modern city life, the ugliness of landscapes and cityscapes surrounding us, unpleasant people, and the noises of "civilization". These are all prominent features. Every time a siren wails or another car drives by, or a bulldozer dozes, the soundtrack increases in volume. By contrast we hear the birds and the wild dogs and other natural sounds such as thunder and rain throughout the film as well.

CW: I noticed there is no musical score in the film (until the final scene, that is) and wondered why.

HE: Again, the director did not want to manipulate his audience's emotions. Without giving musical clues as to what emotions we should be feeling, an audience is free to come to its own conclusions.

128

CW: So what about the conclusion? Why does Mr. K bring us all the way to the end, to the scene where Badii lies in his grave in the rain, only to have the screen go black? Why, then cut to a grainy, camcorder shot of the director and film crew? Isn't that disrupting the flow of what audiences would expect in a concluding scene? We have come all this way, became involved with Badii's narrative, only to find that the climactic build up provides no relief. We feel suffocated, in a sense, and instead are faced with the reality that, yes, we are watching a film, and the entire film has been a construct of the director's imagination. Why does he end the film this ambiguous way?

HE: Yes, the film is a construct. In this way, you can compare Mr. K's filmmaking to conceptual art. There are no concrete answers, no definite conclusions. The only purpose is to offer the viewer challenging questions, without offering answers, much the same way real life functions. Perhaps Mr. K's intention is for art to become reality. We cannot know for sure. As for the shift from Badii's grave to blackness, I believe the director is referring to death. He has said in an interview that "death is a lack of voice and light," therefore whether Badii dies or not, we can only surmise that the blackout is a form of transition. Perhaps here Badii samples death, just before the camera returns to life and apparently, joyful springtime.

CW: Yes. And next we see the film crew and the director, and you giving your friend, Mr. K the cigarette. And the landscape is in bloom, and the real soldiers seem to be enjoying themselves on the hillside. We hear Louis Armstrong's adaptation of 'St. James Infirmary' by trumpet. Doesn't this suggest a funeral march in some cultures? What are we to make of this?

HE: Mr. K has indicated that he chose this song because of its ambiguity, although that point could be argued. It is both a mournful song of death and loss, and it is also a celebration of life. The two may exist simultaneously. Again, the audience decides how to respond.

CW: I have one final question. If your character, Mr. Badii is in such despair, why does he take so long to find just the right person to make sure he is dead and buried properly? Surely one of the thugs at the beginning of the film would have served his purpose? Why does he take so much time interviewing the various characters? Is he trying to find a sympathetic soul to bury him? Another reason?

HE: I believe each character Mr. Badii encounters in the film was chosen for a reason. From the children he sees in the beginning of the film to the rough thugs, to the helpful peasants; each represents a cross-section of humanity. Each of us is faced with the same questions of life and death. Perhaps Badii chose people who might be sympathetic because he really is unsure and wants to be talked out of suicide, yes. Ultimately, in my view the film is about having a choice and having a voice. The reality we face as human beings is increasingly daunting because so many of our choices are dictated by cultural mores and taboos. By using every-day people as actors the director gives us an undistilled version of culture that is embodied in the individual, even as s/he is part of a collective society. Perhaps the human instinct for survival stems from our spiritual and intellectual nature. Even in the depths of sadness or despair, we may still see a glimmer of light at the end of the tunnel when we remember the taste of cherry.

CW: Thank you Mr. Ershadi. It's been a pleasure.

ACKNOWLEDGMENTS

I'd like to thank my father, who introduced me to film at a very early age. From Buck Rogers to Hitchcock and Vincent Price films, to Bergman and Dracula, all the art-house films (*Cat People*, *Koyaanisquatsi*, *Das Boot*), to *Tarzan* and film noir, romance, foreign, and adventure films. Together we've shared this love of movies which I'll carry with me always.

Much gratitude goes to my family and closest friends, who have patiently waited for this writing phase to pass (I wish there were more hours in the day so I could spend them with you).

I would also like to thank my editor-collaborator, Norman, whose artistic "eye" and conceptual influences can be found throughout the book.

Thanks to Eckhard Gerdes for his moral support, to James Hugunin for his smokin' introduction, and lastly, to Black Scat Books.

Round up the usual suspects, it's gonna be a bumpy night!

ABOUT THE AUTHOR

Carla M. Wilson received an MFA in Fiction and has a B.A. in Communications. Her writing and visuals have appeared in *Talking Writing*, *Fiction International*, *Black Scat Review*, *Poetry International*, *Sleipnir*, and *Le Scat Noir*, among others. She lives in San Diego, California.

Selected
BLACK SCAT BOOKS

I AM SARCEY
Alphonse Allais

HERE LIES MEMORY: A Pittsburgh Novel
Doug Rice

THE DETECTIVE WHO DIDN'T HAVE A CLUE
Alain Arias-Misson

SUPERMAN IN AMERICA & OTHER ABSURD PLAYS
Mark Axelrod

SLEEPYTIME CEMETERY: 40 STORIES
Doug Skinner

SWEET AND VICIOUS
Suzanne Burns

SISTER CARRIE CAME
Tom Bussmann

A DAMSEL IN DISTRESS
P. G. Wodehouse

MISSING MYSTERIES
Derek Pell

THE ZOMBIE OF GREAT PERU
Pierre-Corneille Blessebois

WHEN I GROW UP & OTHER MANTRAS
Terri Lloyd

CROCODILE SMILES: SHORT SHRIFT FICTIONS
Yuriy Tarnawsky

SACRED SINS
John Diamond-Nigh

THE STRAW THAT BROKE
Tom Whalen

IMPOSSIBLE CONVERSATIONS
Carla M. Wilson

THREE PLAYS BY ECKHARD GERDES

THE DOUG SKINNER SONGBOOK
Doug Skinner

VAHAZAR
Stanisław Ignacy Witkiewicz

www.ingramcontent.com/pod-product-compliance
Lightning Source LLC
Chambersburg PA
CBHW030523260626
47157CB00005B/1858